W. M. Ramsay

Impressions of Turkey During Twelve Years' Wanderings

W. M. Ramsay

Impressions of Turkey During Twelve Years' Wanderings

ISBN/EAN: 9783337188405

Printed in Europe, USA, Canada, Australia, Japan

Cover: Foto ©Andreas Hilbeck / pixelio.de

More available books at **www.hansebooks.com**

Impressions of Turkey

During Twelve Years' Wanderings

BY

W. M. Ramsay, D.C.L., LL.D.

PROFESSOR IN ABERDEEN UNIVERSITY
FORMERLY FELLOW OF EXETER AND OF LINCOLN COLLEGE, AND
PROFESSOR OF CLASSICAL ARCHÆOLOGY, OXFORD

LONDON
HODDER AND STOUGHTON
27 PATERNOSTER ROW
1897

TO THE MANY FRIENDS

OF MANY NATIONALITIES

WHO HAVE HELPED MY WORK

IN ASIA MINOR

AND ESPECIALLY TO

MR. E. PURSER

AND THE OTHER OFFICIALS OF

THE OTTOMAN RAILWAY

PREFACE

Love for Asiatic Turkey and its people, combined with hope for its future and interest in its past history, may justify the publication of these pages, in which I have tried to record frankly the impressions left on my mind during the wanderings of twelve years, and the studies of seventeen years. I cannot hope that they will be generally acceptable to those whose minds are made up on one side or the other, for they steer a middle course and regard no person and no people as wholly in the right. The method followed is for the most part to take the reader into the heart of Turkey and let him look for himself, explaining my own impression about the facts which he sees.

I began to travel with a strong belief in the imperial mission of Britain, and I end with a stronger faith in the English-speaking race. But I have learned also to appreciate the high qualities of other great nations.

During five years, 1880-1884, my wife and I were resident (or rather nomadic) in Turkey, and after that date, many of my vacations, and some of hers, were devoted to travelling there.   Sir Charles Wilson trained me as an explorer, during two journeys ; and to his wide knowledge of Turkey, Syria and Arabia I am deeply indebted.   But he must not be held in any way responsible for, or sympathetic with, my views.   Except where an authority is quoted, I have studiously avoided borrowing from the conversation and opinions of Western observers, for it seems to me both unfair and misleading to give as one's own impressions of Turkey mere fragments of the talk one has had with other Europeans.

The lessons learned from Sir C. Wilson I passed on to better men than myself, who went with me as beginners in Turkish travel, Mr. A. C. Blunt in Oct.-Nov., 1881, Prof. J. R. S. Sterrett, Amherst College, Mass., in 1883, Mr. A. H. Smith, of the British Museum, in 1884, Mr. H. A. Brown, of Exeter College (who has found in Mashonaland a soldier's death, as one of the thirty-three picked men who composed Major Wilson's ill-fated party), in 1886 and 1887, Mr. D. G. Hogarth, Fellow of Magdalen College, in 1887 and 1890, and the Rev. A. C. Headlam, Fellow of All Souls' College, in 1890. Of these Prof. Sterrett, in 1884, 1885, and Mr. Hogarth, in 1891, 1892, went on to make independent and brilliantly successful journeys in Asia Minor. Mr. Hogarth's *Wandering Scholar in the Levant* gives a vivid and amusing picture of some of his experiences : he has less love for the Turkish peasants than I have, and none of my belief in their capacity for development, while he admires the Turkish officials much more than I do, applying to them, on p. 140, the language which M. Waddington uses of the Roman officers of the best period. His book, with its admiration for the activity and resolution of the Turkish officials, may serve as a corrective to my contempt for their sluggishness and weakness. His view remains a marvel to me.

The Turkish language I have picked up

only in a conversational way from the peasants ; but, though I do not profess to be very familiar with it, yet, in comparison with the ordinary archæologists, I have some considerable advantage. In 1881 I used a Greek interpreter. After 1882 I employed none, but acted as interpreter for my travelling companions.

Some references are made to discussions which I have published elsewhere, in order to suggest that the brief statements sometimes made in these pages on great questions are not set down without thought.

We at first intended to add a chapter on " Turkish Village Life in a Woman's View "; but judged it better to make this into a separate little book, which will, I hope, appear in October, under the auspices of the same publishers.

W. M. RAMSAY.

ABERDEEN, 10th May, 1897.

CONTENTS

CONTENTS

CHAPTER VII.

CHAPTER VIII.

CHAPTER IX.

CHAPTER X.

CHAPTER XI.

CHAPTER XII.

CHAPTER I.

IN A TURKISH VILLAGE OF CENTRAL ANATOLIA.[1]

IT is not difficult to write an interesting description
of an eastern country, if you have spent only a few
months in it.   In that time you see the picturesque
facts ; the salient features of the country, the people,
and the life, impress themselves on you, and group
themselves in a strong, emphatic, unified, well-
conceived picture.   You have learned how simple
oriental life and character are ; how easy it is to
govern an oriental race ; how small a matter it is to
understand the " Eastern Question " ; how quickly
you would clear up the tangle of the Turkish difficulty,
if you had the opportunity.   You can describe the
whole nature of the people in broad, firm, striking
outlines.   You have not been troubled with con-
tradictory impressions, for you have had no time
to receive them.   You have seen only one side,
and the novelty and interest of your experiences

[1] The opening paragraphs of this chapter spring from my own
experience, and have been in my mind as an introduction ever
since 1884, when I began to think of writing this book. They
have no relation to any work except my own.

have impressed that side so strongly on you, that you are filled with the consciousness of new knowledge and the power that it gives, with the conviction of truth in your knowledge. The East, which was only a dream and a theory to you, has become a reality, and you understand all that part of the world's literature that is connected with the East in a way that you never understood it before. You feel what a great step you have made when you came in contact with Eastern men, and appreciated the subtle charm which the oriental nature always exercises on the Western man, if at all imaginative and impressionable. You have learned, too, how absolutely divided is the Eastern man from the Western in all his thoughts and aspirations. You have experienced the impassable gulf that divides you from the oriental, as well as the strange attraction that he exercises on you.

But when the months have grown into years of acquaintance, you don't find the Eastern nature and the "Eastern Question" so easy to understand. You have had time to see more, and you find that every one of your earliest impressions is contradicted by some later experience, that every statement which you formerly made without hesitation has become more doubtful. You can no longer make broad and sweeping assertions and generalisations, for you feel that they are always unfair to some extent, and untrue to some of your knowledge. When you have had a wide enough experience, you can strike an average among your facts ; but even then you can no longer feel that delightful confidence which sweeps you on from fact to fact and carries the reader with you.

As I try to describe the impressions that many journeys have made on me, I feel that the question is likely to be put,—what business has an archæologist to write about modern life and modern manners in Turkey? I have never studied the " Eastern Question ". I went out to Turkey without any intention to do so, filled only with the intense and overmastering desire to understand the old history of the country which has always been the battle-field between the Oriental and the Western spirit. For years I had as a student at college been fascinated with the idea of that long conflict which is the epitome of all history, the battle of East and West ; and now I was going to the land that stretches like a bridge from the East to the West, connecting them at once and separating them. To understand and sympathise with the spirit of the land was my only thought.

It is, however, perhaps no disadvantage that I did not go out to study the " Eastern Question ". Half an hour's talk with a man who is going out for that purpose is usually enough to show you pretty clearly what answer he will bring back. According to his sympathies and prejudices will be the company in which he is plunged and the information that he receives. He will return feeling more strongly than ever that he was right from the beginning. I was saved from that fate by the fact that my sole guide and my sole criterion in all circumstances was the wish to learn about past history. I went where I could learn and forced everybody to teach me. I did not go to look for walls, and columns, temples, and statues, and coins. Many cities and monuments have been before my eyes, but I do not pose as their discoverer. What I hope is, with the help of many men and many minds, to have thought over them, till I have gained a true idea of the people who built them and the society which needed them.

But for my purposes it was necessary that new evidence, in other words unknown monuments, should be discovered ; and the practical problem of discovery in Asia Minor always presents itself as a study in human nature. You come in contact with all classes of the native population, Moslem and Christian, Jews and Kizil-Bash, and you must observe and adapt yourself to the character and prejudices of every one, if you want to make many discoveries. If you go into a village, and ask point blank whether there are any " written stones " (*yasili tashlar*) or "marbles" (*mermer*, distinguished from common stones, *kara-tash*) or "old money" (*eski para*), every man is ready to swear that there is nothing of the kind : in other villages at a distance, three or five or ten hours away, they know that there is abundance of such things, but here there is nothing whatsoever. You may point to a "written marble" in the fountain beside which you have halted ; but you are told that it has been brought from far away, and there are no others like it in the village. In the estimation of the villagers, wise from long and sad experience, every stranger who asks questions and whose business is not obvious, must be an agent of the Government, and therefore an enemy ; and their wish and hope and prayer is to get rid of him as quickly and cheaply as possible. It is a lesson in the "Eastern Question" to see the dislike and fear with which every village regards the Government. You are more struck with this in the Mohammedan villages, for, in the Greek villages at least, the Christian people are quicker witted, and can distinguish more readily between the Government agent and the travelling scholar.

Your archæologist takes a less direct, but a more fruitful method. Among Mohammedans he does not declare at once his business, for no one would believe in his sincerity (except in some sophisticated villages, where those strange beings that are mad after "written stones" have become familiar in recent years). He stops his horse in the first open space, usually near a fountain or a mosque, a glance at which gives him some idea of the "stone-producing" capacity of the place. In three minutes he is surrounded by the entire male population. Unless it is the harvest season, when the men condescend to do a little work, they have been sitting in some shady place, usually beside or in the "guest-room" (*Musafir-Oda*), talking little, and only at rare intervals, those who can muster up a little tobacco smoking cigarettes, which they are very generous in sharing with one another. If there is any man of wealth in the village, he has an Oda of his own, where he entertains all comers ; and the more respectable and respected part of the male population is usually congregated there ; the great man smokes his narghile, the rest cigarettes, and the droning sound of the rich man's hubble-bubble adds to the soporific effect of the warm summer weather and the quiet and lazy surroundings.

As the news spreads that a stranger has arrived and is asking for the Musafir-Oda, unwonted bustle reigns in the village. A pleasing, mild excitement affects the population. The loungers in the Oda rise, go to the door, look in the heap of old slippers, down at heel and usually full of holes, for their own property, which they recognise with marvellous intelligence among many that seem to your eyes undistinguishable, slowly slip their feet into them, and then as slowly shuffle their way to where the archæologist is sitting on his horse. All are eager to ask the traditional series of questions, like the Cyclops in the Odyssey, "Where do you come from? What is your business? Where are you going to?" You do not too hastily gratify their curiosity, but leave them in pleasant anticipation while you inquire for the Oda. If there is a rich man who keeps his own Oda, you have already contrived to pick up this information from some casual wayfarer, who has arrested his wandering step at sight of the strangers; and you flatter the local swell by asking for his Oda, showing your familiarity with his name and his reputation for hospitality.

The whole company then goes away to the Oda; the archæologists leave their horses to their servants, go in and sit down in the place of honour, the host or headman of the village does the same, and each salutes the other. If you are prudent, you throw your waterproof on the mats or cushions before you take up your position; for the cushions and carpets are always full of dust and fleas, and vermin loathe waterproof, while it also prevents the dust from rising. After every one has sat

down and saluted, and there is a general atmosphere of expectation, the questions as to your
origin and destination are repeated; and you pro-
ceed by degrees to gratify the general curiosity.
Your business is to amuse and interest the people.
Their life is spent in an atmosphere of monotony,
amid a regular alternation of the annual incidents
of winter, sowing time and harvest, where the occasional visit of an official is the only great trouble,
and the rare visit of a stranger furnishes the only
entertainment. If you want to get from them the
information which you desire, you must pay for it
by giving them as much pleasure and excitement
as you can; and it is important to study the best
ways of catching the interest and sympathy of
your villagers. You tell them you come from
England, from London (*Inghilterra-dann, Londra-
dann*); and you answer as seems best the almost
invariable question, " Whether is England in London, or London in England?" You tell that
London is the principal city of Inghilterra, but
there are other cities there besides; and there is a
little buzz of stage-whispering, as each imparts to
his neighbour the news that you come from Londra, the head city, and must therefore be a man of
real consequence. No one but a " tenderfoot "
will say that he comes from any second-rate place,
like Oxford: if he does, he sets himself down as a

mere villager like themselves, and sinks correspondingly in their estimation.

During the conversation you pass round a supply of tobacco, and every villager rolls himself a cigarette. On their side the entertainers prepare coffee:[1] one of their number makes a little fire on the hearth, produces some coffee beans from some receptacle in the room or from the person of the local magnate, roasts them, grinds them, boils the water in a little high narrow tin pot with a long handle, pours in the fine-ground powder, allows the coffee to come twice to the boiling point, and then pours it into two or three small cups, which are offered first to the guests. If there is a lady among the guests, sometimes one of the Turks who has seen more of the world directs the bearer to offer to the lady first; if not it is wise to sign to him yourself to do so. The unusual order imparts more interest in the general esteem: it is much for them to see a stranger of quaint dress and manners; it is an even greater novelty that a lady should travel and talk and sit in the company of men; but, when the male guest, a person attended by servants, and obviously possessing wealth beyond the dreams of

[1] It is said that true oriental etiquette requires that no questions should be put to the stranger till coffee has been offered to him. That has not been my experience among villagers; in more cultivated society coffee is offered at once, but it takes a long time to get it ready in a village.

avarice, orders the lady to be served first, it becomes clear to the least instructed villager that she
must be a very great person indeed, far above the
ordinary restraints of her sex, probably a near relative of the Sultan of Inghilterra. Then some one
brings forth a tale which he has heard somewhere,
that it is the custom in Inghilterra to have a woman
as supreme ruler; and the question is propounded,
whether this is really true. A short sketch of the
British constitution, adapted to the comprehension
of the audience, is useful and effective at this stage.

Then you begin to talk about themselves, for to
every man the most interesting subject is himself,
and it is the greatest of consolations to him to talk
freely about his grievances. You inquire about the
prospects of the coming harvest or the last visit of
the tax-gatherer, and sympathise with the invariable
tale of rapacity, injustice and cruelty on the part of
the officials. You hear how old men have been ill-
treated or imprisoned, how many peasants have
had their oxen for ploughing seized and sold, how
much the taxes have increased in recent years.

Now comes the archæologist's opportunity, when
mutual confidence is established. He introduces
the subject of "old stones" and " antikas ". The
guileless villagers rush headlong into the harmless
trap; every one is eager to tell what he knows;
and we sally forth in a body. Even the local

great man is sometimes roused to such unwonted activity as to rise and walk round with the rest ; if you have any distance to go, you are wise to offer him the use of one of your servants' horses, and the stirrups will require no adjustment to suit him ; for all Turks tall or little ride with the same stirrup.   One man has got a " written stone " at the side of his fire-place, another in the wall of his house, a third has seen one in a field outside the town.   You pay with prudently ostentatious liberality for the first, before you copy it ; and the general eagerness to find inscriptions is increased tenfold.   After that the men of the village are ready to dig up every tombstone in the cemeteries (which usually occupy more space than the dwelling-houses), if there be any prospect of finding letters on one.   But the women are not so easy to deal with, and, if news is carried out to the fields that some infidel dogs are desecrating the cemetery, they sometimes rush in, hot and wild with excitement, and the scene becomes lively.   Do not be too much impressed with their pious respect for the graves of their ancestors, for other motives co-operate with that praiseworthy feeling in their minds.   Either they have not heard or they have not believed that the Giaours are paying in good silver for looking at the stones.   Moreover they know that your real object is to get the gold that is concealed within those stones ; and, if the men are silly enough to sell gold for silver, they are resolved to know the reason why, even though the usual restraints of the sex have to be for a time thrown off. The men are convinced by them, for the Mohammedan mind can never fully believe that a man travels for any other object than gold : if Christianity had done nothing else in the East, it would be a great achievement that it has enabled simple villagers to believe that men can travel from mere desire of knowledge, and work for mere ideals. When matters in the village get to this stage, and every one makes up his mind that you are searching for gold, relations are sometimes imperilled ; and, as it is useless further to deny that gold is your aim, the best way is to promise to give to all a fair share of whatever is found, and to urge them to co-operate and to keep strict watch on their neighbours and on yourself.

Many are the exclamations of wonder, *Mash-allah!* "What God wills!" as the archæological note-book is produced, and the letters copied into it. If the inscription is upside down, as it is in the majority of cases, your contortions as you struggle to get into a position to see it, cause much interest ; and, really, it is no wonder that the natives believe all Ingleez to be mad, as they see you trying to stand on your head and write in a book at the same time, especially as you have tried to make them believe that you do this for no advantage to yourself, but purely for pleasure.

If the inscription is important enough to deserve an impression, that is a great time for the village, as you demand water, dip in the impression paper; this is obviously a spell to facilitate the discovery of the treasure hid within the stone, and every one gazes in breathless attention. The natives, however, are sadly disappointed when, after some hours or days of work, the archæologist departs no richer that he came; but the marvel grows with time, and the next traveller who comes a few years later, will probably hear that you departed with several camels' load of treasure. Several times a servant of mine, arriving before me at a village, has heard wonderful tales of this kind about a traveller; and on my arrival I have been recognised as the hero of these fables.

The process, as thus described, seems tedious; and it is not every one who will go through it. But the first lesson one has to learn in the East is that time has no value; and, if you are in a hurry, you will never get on so well with the Orientals. Prof. Sterrett had great power of suiting himself to the natives, and true sympathy with them; and I did not appreciate how much he had done for me by these qualities, till I observed some other explorers, who with many admirable and splendid qualities as travellers, had not the sympathy and the patience that are required for scenes like this. But I would urge upon all archæological travellers how important it is to study the natives, to learn about them direct and not from report of others, to observe and study small things, to give some time and care to the people through whom alone the best discoveries are likely to be made. As reward for a little patience and sympathy and kindliness, you learn something of the thoughts and life of a very simple-minded and interesting people, and you may go away rich in historic treasure, better able to interpret the monuments that you have discovered, ready to write a new page of history, or to give fresh colour and clearness to the tale of St. Paul's wanderings.

CHAPTER II.

IT is then a useful part of the archæologist's education that he should learn to interest and amuse the simple-minded audiences which surround and gaze upon him in a Turkish village. You find by experience some little jokes, which suit the native wit; and you may be sure that the remark which proves effective in one Turkish village will be equally suitable in all. Every one must learn what suits his own style. One little remark which I first made in sheer despair, proved immensely effective; and, when well introduced afterwards on many an occasion, never failed to " bring down the house ". After a considerable conversation, in which I had been inquiring about the roads, the distances, the course of the streams, and other geographical points, in respect of which I possessed a certain ease and fluency in Turkish, a native took the lead, and began to question me in a more thorough-going way than is usual. He soon exhausted my small stock of Turkish; and at last, being quite nonplussed by a long explana-

(15)

tory question, I exclaimed, "*Turktche bilmaiorim*" (I don't know Turkish). Every one saw through this barefaced excuse: that a man who had been talking with perfect fluency for a quarter of an hour, so long as he was the questioner, and had been draining them of information about the natural features and lie of the country, should try to evade their questions by pretending not to know Turkish! they were too acute to be taken in by chaff like this: every one, proud of his own perspicacity, turned to his neighbour, nudged him in the ribs to attract his attention, imparted to him the information that the stranger was a deep and artful dodger, but they were too smart for him, and saw through his stratagems. Pleased with their own acuteness, they become pleased with you.

Another unfailing way of delighting the natives is to draw a pointed and judicious contrast between the English and the Turkish character. You take your text from the wonder which they always feel that a millionaire like yourself should go through so much fatigue as you submit to every day; and you explain that in Inghilterra, when a man possesses money he goes away to travel and visits many lands and peoples, while the poor man stays at home; but in Turkey, when a man is rich, he sits in his house, and only the poor man goes forth to work. Your remarks, if well put to them, rouse intense interest, sometimes almost laughter (your Turk does not often laugh) at your picture of Turkish nature; and occasionally it is clear that you have succeeded in making them think a little.

In 1883 Prof. Sterrett and I went to Orkistos, on the frontier of Galatia, to look for a great inscription, which had been apparently lost. It had been seen and copied unsatisfactorily by several old travellers, last of all by Hamilton. In 1861 the Berlin Academy instructed Dr. Mordtmann to recopy it; but he failed to discover it. As Mordtmann was familiar with the Turkish language and an experienced traveller, the discovery was obviously no easy matter; and some care was needed. We arranged our journey so as to sleep at a village some hours distant, and next morning came on to Alikel (earlier travellers call the place Alekian). Here we found ourselves at a Turkmen Yaila, in a splendid situation, with fertile lands, abundance of water and grass, and a profusion of inscribed stones. We avoided showing any interest in these, but intimated our intention of inviting all the leading men to dinner, and proceeded to purchase a sheep which was to be cooked entire by the villagers for their own benefit. I took means to find out whether they preferred a lamb of that year, or a full-grown sheep (whose flesh to us would have been uneatable):

their opinion was conveyed almost in the words of
the poet :—

> A one-year sheep was sweeter,
>   But a two-year sheep was fatter ;
> Therefore they thought it meeter
>   To feed upon the latter.

After this was arranged, and the sheep and cooks
selected, we went away to see the winter village
(*Kishla*) and the river Sangarios, as it seemed
better not to show interest in antiquities at this
stage. In the evening our Turkish servant pre-
sided at the dinner, and turned the conversation on
Mordtmann's visit : several of those present remembered him and his vain inquiries after the
stone, whose situation they willingly described.
Next morning a great crowd came to the mill with
us, and showed where the stone was hidden : it
formed the main support at the end of an embankment along which the stream was conducted to
turn the mill. It was easy to strike a bargain with
the miller to uncover the stone, for the mill was
not working. A score of willing hands soon pulled
away the loose material ; but, alas ! the water had
deposited a hard thick incrustation which covered
the letters and filled up the hollows, leaving in most
places a smooth surface. Here and there a few
words could be read, so that the inscription was
identified. In a few minutes we recognised that

the stone could not be cleaned with our present equipment; and it seemed better to cover it up forthwith carefully and to show some disappointment, as if the stone had turned out valueless: one might return later after learning at some museum how to clean marble. We spent the rest of the day in copying the other inscriptions, especially one large and difficult stone, and enjoying the delightful air and the hospitable kindness of the Turkmens.

To finish the history of that inscription, the " Charter of Orkistos," in February, 1884, I went to Berlin, where Professor Conze, keeper of the Royal Museum, allowed me to see the process of cleaning the Pergamenian marbles: but it was not till 1886 that A. H. Brown and I, returning from Cappadocia along the Halys and through Angora, took Orkistos on our way. We came from Sivri-Hissar, seven hours distant, intending to reach Alikel for lunch; but were detained till afternoon. In order to have the opportunity of using some show of authority, if need be, we brought a *zaptieh* with us, to whom I promised a pound, as soon as the stone was fairly in our hands in a suitable position with full freedom for copying; but he was instructed to do nothing at first except praise our high rank and. influence. We found that the large stone over which Sterrett and I spent so much time in 1883 had been broken immediately after our departure in order to find the gold that we had obviously been seeking for ; but the stone at the mill, which we had regarded with contempt, was uninjured. The miller had his mill going ; I think he suspected our object, and set the water on as soon as we rode into the Yaila, with the object of raising the price. It did not, however, take much time to conclude a bargain, for it was cheaper to pay a pound or two extra, than to waste time or risk failure. Before sunset, we had the end of the embankment demolished, and the great stone laid flat on the grass beside it, to do as we pleased with. The miller rebuilt the embankment with other stones : but did not use the mill, having apparently no need for working after the bargain was concluded. It took four days' work, with the tools that I had brought from Berlin, to clean the stone, and copy the inscription. The Berlin authorities recognised the service by a letter of thanks from the Minister of Education, and a liberal contribution to the expenses of the expedition.

Probably an archæologist who could do some easy sleight of hand tricks would have a great advantage as a discoverer. Certainly, a few children's picture books would be a great resource, and furnish unfailing amusement to the natives ; and even more effective would be the art which with scissors clips a menagerie of animals out of a sheet or two of paper.   Childish pleasures like that would exactly suit the Turkish villagers, for, intellectually, they are only children.   In the quiet unbroken monotony of village life, they make no mental growth.   The even placidity of Turkish village life is hardly credible.   Round a Christian or a Circassian village, there is at least a variety of crops ; vegetables of several kinds are grown ; butter is made ; and a certain amount of art and work is expended in giving variety and interest to food and to life.   But the one duty of the Turkish man originally was to be a soldier ; and when he is not seized by the conscription or compelled by poverty and debt to go to Smyrna or Stambol or a railway line, where money can be earned, he lounges through life doing absolutely nothing, fed by the women, occasionally crocheting a stocking,[1] or minding a little child of two or three years old. As all field work falls to the share of the women, in addition to most of the house-work (of which however the total amount is but small), cultivation is restricted to the simplest operations.   Enough of corn is sown to feed the village, and nothing more is produced.   The villagers feed on little except bread, with thick sour milk (a delightful adjunct to food in hot weather) ; meat is not common except

[1] That is the process, not knitting, as Mrs. Ramsay pointed out to me.

on high days and holidays; though the richer
Turks are often great eaters.

Every one of the few processes in Turkey that
require skilled labour is performed by a Christian.
If a Turk lives in anything better built than a hut,
I have always found that it is constructed by a
Greek. If a Turkish village requires a fountain
with its aqueduct, a Greek workman is employed
to make it. On a splendid Seljuk *medresse*
(religious college) at Sivas is inscribed the name of
the Greek architect Kalo-Yannis. Needless to say
that almost all trade, especially the carrying and
retail trade, is in the hands of Christians: the
muleteer is often, and the camel-driver always,
Turk or Turkmen, but the owner both of the goods
and of the animals is a Christian. The Turk, if he
works, is a servant, a hewer of wood and a drawer
of water: he rarely can learn to do more. Only in
certain districts, where some manufacture has been
practised from time immemorial, do you find Turks
engaged in it; but the careful observer will entertain no doubt that they are only the older population
Mohammedanized. At Tyana I found an able and
active and wealthy Turk; but he was distinctly not
Turk in type or race.

Life is thus reduced to its simplest elements and
the most unvaried uniformity. A company of
Turks in a village will sit for hours in almost

unbroken silence. I happened once in early October, 1883, to come to a village, Tatarli, in the Tchul-Ova, late in the afternoon, after a fatiguing and disappointing day. I was making an experimental journey, in an economical way, accompanied by a single Turkish servant and a led horse to carry our belongings. The experiment was an utter failure, as will be duly set forth in chapter xii., and I had on that day realised finally that it was a failure, but that it must go on for a fortnight longer. Being in a dull and languid humour, I was disinclined for the strain of talking to and amusing the usual assemblage of gazers at the Oda; and thought the procedure might be profitably varied by trying how long they would remain silent. Except for a few words and questions on the part of my man, Murad, when he wanted water, chopped straw for the horses, and our other simple requirements, no one spoke. I worked languidly at my route survey. Murad was even more sick of this one-horse style of travelling than I was, and was probably affected by my dulness, for in general he was good company. He looked after the horses, cooked our dinner of *bulgur*-pilaff, of which I ate a little, while the circle gazed and meditated.

> Muckle we looked, and muckle we thocht,
> But word we ne'er spak' nane.

Then Murad got out my blankets, and found in the Oda a very old and thin mattress, which served to keep the hard floor from my bones, while a waterproof spread over it prevented its inhabitants from reaching my skin. It was now about three hours since we entered the village, and about two and a half since any one had spoken. I made my preparations for the night, disrobed myself, performed my simple ablutions, and got in between the blankets. Everybody gazed, and admired, and wondered what should come next. A lighted lamp hung from the roof. I sat up and blew it out. Then, at last, the leading magnate of the village remarked, " Now let us go " (*Kshimdi gidelim*), and they left me alone. I think they were a little chilled and depressed, for, next morning, hardly any one came to see us breakfast.

Again in 1884, returning to camp after being detained from it by distance the preceding night, I was seized with fever, when there was still two hours' journey before us. As we were near a village we went into it, and as the Oda was not fit to use, from some cause or other, I lay down on the shady side of a wall, while my servant put up my horse, and then rode off to camp with orders to bring me a kettle, some tea, and some quinine. I waited alone ; a score of villagers came and sat round in a semicircle ; I doubt if any of us moved a muscle till the medicines arrived, two or three hours later.

The British Consul at Angora in 1882, Mr. Gatheral, a Glasgow man, who died shortly after our visit, told us a very characteristic story of Turkish habits. Stevens, the first cyclist to make an excursion round the world, had passed through Angora a year or two previously. His arrival on one of the old lofty "bone-shakers" caused immense excitement, and his departure on the following day was made a public ceremony. A great crowd, including, I think, the Vali-Pasha himself, assembled at the city gate from which he started, and it was arranged that a cannon should be fired as he mounted, partly as a signal to the crowds of gazers along the road, partly, perhaps, as a compliment to him. A number of Turks collected at a wayside coffee-house a mile or more up the winding road that leads towards the East. They waited till the gun fired, then they all rose up, each selected his own shoes among the pile that lay at the door, shuffled his way into his shoes, and then shuffled to the roadside a few yards from the house, and sat down to wait till the strange machine with one wheel arrived. They sat for an hour, and began to think there was some delay. They sat for another hour, and then some of them began to drop off to other pressing concerns. The majority, however, sat on in patient expectation. But they never saw Stevens. He had shot past them while they were engaged in shuffling on their shoes.

In dealing with Orientals, a prime necessity is perfect straight-forwardness and transparent honesty: there should never be the slightest variation in your word at different times or between your word and your act. What you have once said should be final and irrevocable: be it wise or foolish in itself, you should never draw back from it or reconsider it: and when you realise this, you become careful and think several times before deciding. Even in offering money for a coin or antique of any kind, I made a rule never to vary from my first offer to a Turk; if he tried to bargain, it was explained to him that I "had only one word"; I had stated the value, and it was for him to choose whether he wanted the money or not. Of course, this way often caused the loss of a coin, which a more skilful bargainer would have bought; but it produced a great impression on the Turks, and everything that inspires them with respect helps the traveller's purpose; and (to one who has none of the collector's instinct, and gathers from the type and legend all the evidence that he seeks for) coins are of no consequence except as means to attract people and make them interested.

In conversation at home, wonder is often expressed that I could have avoided smoking, while travelling so long in Turkey. But in Turkey I often overheard the account given by my men of my character and rank: among the first qualities stated was "he drinks no coffee: he drinks no tobacco:[1] he drinks no raki". To drink coffee, and not to drink tobacco, as I did in the earlier years of travelling, is a proof of folly or weakness; but to drink nothing is a mark of great virtue. As wine or raki can be procured only at a few great cities, strict temperance is compulsory for the archæologist travelling; but my experience as to the effect on his working powers is unfavourable. Coming in exhausted from a long day's work in the sun, and eating in this condition, I could not sleep for many hours; but a small glass of raki before eating, if procurable, was a medicine that always ensured a good sleep. Of course one ought not to work to exhaustion; but that prudent rule is easy to give and hard to follow. In the later journeys I did not work so hard; but it was different when I was beginning, and success was far ahead.

An important rule of conduct among the Turks is that you must never permit the slightest sign of

[1] To drink tobacco is the term for smoking both in Turkish and Greek.

disrespect to pass. Point it out at once ; insist on redress ; and you will always be obeyed, if it is clear that you mean business. It needs, of course, both natural sense, sympathy, and some knowledge of the people and manners, to discriminate between well-meant manners, different from ours, and actual disrespect. Some things are intended for compliments, which we do not fully appreciate at their intended value, as when a man insists on helping you by peeling your hard-boiled egg with his dirty fingers : you may acknowledge the courtesy and lay aside the egg. But it is better to be too strict, than to pass over anything that may be disrespectful. When in doubt, strike ! That is the golden rule in Turkey. You must speak and act as one having authority.

Several of the older travellers in Turkey suffered from not observing this rule. Hamilton, in his earlier journeys, speaks several times of the annoyance to which he was exposed. In vol. i., p. 193, for example, he says : " To our disappointment, the house belonged to a Turk : we always preferred a Greek or Armenian house, in which we were less exposed to the inconvenient and sometimes impertinent curiosity of the host : in this case, however, the ill-timed curiosity of our landlord, who at once began pulling about and scrutinising the military buttons of my companion's coat, met with a suitable rebuff from the colonel, who had no idea at the time that the man was not one of the servants of the house ".

Hamilton travelled in 1831, when the Turks had not been tamed by adversity ; and he seems to have found them very ready to air their fancied superiority to one or two slenderly equipped European travellers. Older travellers often give the same report. Macdonald Kinneir, in 1813, speaks of " that blustering air so peculiar to Turks "; but his adventure at Eski-Sheher gives such a bad picture of his way of dealing with Orientals that one cannot wonder at his experiences being unfortunate.[1] In several other cases the travellers were obviously so ignorant of everything, and so anxious and timid, that one can set little store by their impressions of native character : a man may look very fierce and dangerous, with a shaggy moustache and quite a museum of lethal weapons adorning his person, and yet be most reasonable and good-humoured when you address him in a courteous style, and if you put a touch of authority and confidence into it, so much the better.

An experienced traveller, Mr. Barkley, in his *Ride through Asia Minor*, p. 83, says very justly : " All village Turks talk well for ignorant people, and when paying you a visit behave quietly and well. They

[1] *Journey through Asia Minor* pp. 32 and 40.

will talk of horses, game, soldiering, farming, etc. ; and from them the traveller may pick up a good deal of useful information. But in these days (1878), sooner or later the conversation is sure to turn upon the iniquity of the ruling classes, and the Sultan, the Grand Vizier, the provincial governors, great and small, all will come in for violent abuse ; and, as the same story is told in each village, it becomes monotonous."

It is, of course, an absolute necessity to avoid touching their deep-lying feelings as regards religion, family life, and women. But if you feel in your own heart a real sympathy for the people and respect for what is best in them, you will never find it necessary even to consciously think about how to avoid violating their feelings on these subjects (except in cases of sudden change to a different and strange race, as on p. 120). No rule can be given except to feel sympathetic, but no other rule is needed, if you feel so.

Most of what I have to say on these subjects belongs to the period before the recent Mohammedan revival [1] had begun, or at least before it affected the villagers. A serious change has been prepared and brought about by degrees ; and I am fully prepared to learn that the archæologist's trade has become a much harder one. And, as

[1] See chapter vii.

these lines are going through the press, the war with Greece increases enormously the Mohammedan reaction, and embitters relations between Christian and Moslem. The expulsion and actual deportation of Greek subjects from Turkey, if it be carried out completely, will produce a profound effect in many ways. To take one single instance, many of the officials of middle rank on the Ottoman Railway are Greek subjects; and, if they be all expelled, it will be difficult to run the trains on the line.

In respect of religious feeling or intolerance there is a marked contrast between the village Turks and the city Turks. In the villages you rarely see any signs of bigotry or of dislike to Christians. The people seemed never to have the slightest objection to my going freely about their mosques; and, when I asked whether I need take off my shoes, they generally assured me that it was quite unnecessary. For a small consideration, a dollar or two, they will permit the archæologist to make an excavation beside the mosque, or to saw away part of a plank in the floor, when an inscription is concealed under the soil or the wooden flooring. Naturally, there must be a certain delicacy shown in the preliminaries; you find out who is the man of most weight and influence in the village, and talk to him privately; you make it clear to him that there will be no real harm done to the building, that the soil removed can be put back again so that no one will know the difference, or that the piece of plank which you want to saw away is close to the wall and the want of it will never be noticed; and the objections, which he makes at first, all disappear when you give him a small coin and show him the larger sum which shall be his, as soon as the obstacle is removed. He will manage the other villagers. The women are harder to deal with; and, when they are roused (which is only very rarely), the situation becomes complicated, and one must trust to accident and chance for some favourable opening. The man of weight and influence, who could sway the other men with a word, often shrinks and becomes dumb when the women appear; and the code of manners forbids you to negotiate privately with a leader among them. This is one of the difficulties from which the archæologist is saved by his wife's company: the women then become almost always favourable, and in many cases I have got freedom in my wife's company to do what I should hardly have been permitted to do alone.

Too much stress must not be laid on our experience. We were a holiday and a show to the village, like a visit of Wombwell's Menagerie, Barnum's Greatest Show on Earth, or Professor Pepper's

Ghost in a small country town in England. For the time, the village was turned topsy-turvy; the gravest and steadiest heads felt the intoxication of excitement and pleasure-going, combined with the unwonted sensation of money-making; a general spirit of reckless gambling in precious stones seized on everybody; serious elderly men so far forgot themselves as to walk quite at the rate of three and a half miles per hour in search of some promising stone which they remembered. The day would furnish subject of conversation and legend for the rest of their lives. In such circumstances the ordinary restraints of religion were readily overstepped.

Moreover, it is not the deepest feelings that are most readily revealed to passing strangers. And though in 1883, and 1884, I saw life as it is in the Turkish villages a great deal more intimately than archæologists usually see it, and far more intimately than I did as a rule in later years, yet after all it was only a superficial view that I got. The inner life was, of course, concealed from the visitor of a day. There are depths, too, in village life which I have heard about, and which I wished to avoid attempting to plumb. I was not investigating the moral and social condition of the Turks, but seeking for historical evidence; and I had not then realised how much ancient history still remains in Turkey, clothed in Mohammedan forms, and called by

Turkish or Arabic names (ch. xi.).   The traveller must always be careful to avoid concluding that what he has not seen does not exist; though it is strange how little the most superficial travellers recognise that.

Even among the Greek villagers I might in the same way say that I saw few signs of hatred for the Turks, and never among those who spoke only Turkish.   The latter could not be so sure that they were unintelligible to any Turk, even though none could be seen ; moreover, the use of Greek is a bond of sympathy between strangers, which induces confidence.   But, as a rule, in talking with the Greeks of the inner parts of Turkey, we had other business in hand; and I always rather avoided drawing the Christians into conversation about their feelings towards the Turks, for it could do no good, and might lead to complications.   It was almost as rare an experience to hear in a Greek village ex-pressions of hatred to Mohammedans in general, as *vice versa*.   Once in 1883, I found a Greek *bakal* (keeper of a small retail shop or general store) who had started trade in Islam-Keui.   As he was turning away from a group of Turks to show me something, he muttered in a low voice, "abominations of Turks" (*misémata Toúrkón*).   But this was a solitary instance in my experience ; and his words may have been caused by his unfortunate business experience, for trade, even in a large village like Islam-Keui, was very flat. Purchasers were few, and they had no money to pay; promises (or perhaps threats, I cannot say as to that case, but know as regards some cases) were their only coin. In 1883 I again passed through Islam-Keui some months later, and asked for the *bakal*, as Greeks have always better scent for antiquities than Turks. He had given up business in despair: as my man Murad said, "how could a shop exist in a village?" And yet Islam-Keui ought to be a town of great consequence, being the seat of a Mudir, and situated beside the junction of many roads at the entrance to a great pass[1] on one of the great trade-routes of modern Turkey and of all history.

A good example of the easy tolerance of the villagers occurred at Seurlar in the eastern Tchal district, in 1888, when my wife and I were travelling without a tent. It was in Ramazan, the holy month, when fasting throughout the long summer day exalts the religious fervour and sharpens the temper of the Turks; but they welcomed us cordially, entertained us in an open room beside the mosque, inside the sacred precinct, and actually forming part of the sacred building. After their evening meal, the elders assembled there, conversed with us, performed their prayers in chorus before

[1] Described on p. 62.

us ; and at last, when we intimated our wish to rest, they helped our men to hang up carpets across the open side of the room, so that we might be entirely private.

It is strange how religious feeling seems to grow with numbers. It often struck me, sitting among a small group of Turks, that perfect friendliness reigned between us ; but, as more came in, a barrier seemed to grow up, and the gulf between us seemed to become present to the consciousness of all. So in the towns and cities bigotry is far more marked than in the villages. But even in the cities, I have rarely experienced any real difficulty from religious feeling among the Mohammedans. Once I was assaulted with stones, but that was a mere farce. I was riding in 1883 through a singularly unknown, yet not a very remote country, north-east from Tchal, accompanied only by a Greek servant. That is not a good way ; but Prof. Sterrett and I had only one Moslem servant. In one town, which contained a Medresse (religious college), a crowd of boys pursued and began to stone us. No grown-up person showed himself, whom I might have held responsible for the conduct of the boys ; and that in itself was a bad sign of their feeling. I tried by a display of Christian patience to tempt them outside the limits of the town ; but they would not venture beyond the shadow of the last house, and I could only turn and shake my whip in impotent wrath. I felt pretty mad; but it seemed best to ride on and leave the town only half explored, as I had no one but a Christian with me.

Among the more educated and wealthier Turks in the country districts, a few cases came under my notice of sour and arrogant fanaticism and loathing of the Giaours; and, naturally, one observed such cases only where accident brought us into relations with these unpleasing specimens. It is probable, and even certain, that other cases escaped me, because the strict Moslems avoided meeting me. For example, I was several times at a village Tchardak; but only once came into relations with a hard and surly Turk, a man of considerable wealth, and of the strict religious type which is favoured under the present *régime* and is therefore becoming fashionable. It happened in 1888 that my wife and I arrived after a long day's ride, in uncertain and showery weather. We were travelling without a tent; and it was therefore necessary to find a house. All strangers in this village went to the Oda of this rich and religious Turk, for hospitality was a duty to him just as much as prayers. As a general rule, Turks have been specially polite, when an Ingleez lady was in the company; and I was therefore surprised that our host held aloof persistently and avoided bidding us welcome. Inquiring whether the host was absent, I learned that a youngish-looking man, fairly tall, with the white linen band round his fez which had made me take him for the village hodja, was the host. This man had given us the coldest and barest possible salutation, when we entered and sat down : he was one of the new style of Turks, detesting Europeans and all their ways ; when we had, however, come to his house, his religion forbade him to turn us away. We had already eaten food, *viz.*, a fowl supplied by him and cooked by one of our servants ; and he had declined to receive payment, though the man had been ordered to offer it. Had we heard sooner of his character we might have done without anything except the shelter of his roof; the weather, the time of our arrival and the distance of the nearest village made us absolutely dependent on him to that extent. I have never known food so nearly choke me ; and I never spent a night in such annoyance, or was so glad to leave a house. This was the only case in which a Turk was pointedly and studiedly rude to me ; even at the time when the English were most unpopular, in 1883 and 1884, the officials preserved an outward show of politeness while doing a good deal to cause inconvenience ; and any people that may have strongly objected to us contented themselves with ignoring us.

But, in a number of cases, wealthier Turks

showed us cordial hospitality and great attention ; and this was the case chiefly in the remotest and least sophisticated country districts.   It is when he is most unconscious and most natural that the Turk is cordial and charming.   When he begins to try to think, he becomes disagreeable.   Any educative influences that are brought to bear upon the richer class of Turks are, for the most part, either degrading to his character, or calculated to foster arrogance and fanaticism.

Of the city Turks I have hardly any knowledge ; but that fact in itself tells a tale.   In the cities the archæologist hardly ever comes into any relations with the Mohammedans.   The gulf that divides Moslem and Christian is in them difficult to bridge over ; and a casual visitor, coming for a day, has rarely the opportunity of crossing it.[1]   There is much more opportunity of getting into relations with the Mohammedans, if the archæologist's wife accompanies him, for that is a proof of rank and standing and respectability, and, moreover, the rare event of a European lady's advent rouses intense curiosity among the Turkish ladies, and invitations come.   As a general rule, however, my visits to cities were too short and hurried.   There remains much archæological discovery to make in the great cities ; the man who is to make it must have plenty

[1] An exception on p. 291.

of time, and must take with him a wife, possessed of courage, tact, pleasant manners, and the moral power that wins respect without exacting it.

With their simplicity and frankness, the villagers were to me an unfailing pleasure, especially after I learned how to manage the fleas (p. 92). There is great gravity and dignity and courtesy about the middle-aged and elderly men, whom one meets in the Oda. Differences of course exist ; and in some villages people are far better than in others. In this respect the variation is probably due to difference of race. Observant travellers, with a taste for ethnology, might learn a great deal ; but, unfortunately, I did not become alive to this side of my work till near the end.

There was also to me a great charm in the grave, sober, measured intonation of Turkish conversation ; and the language, with its sententiousness, its entire want of relative pronouns and subordinating conjunctions, was full of interest. I know no language which gives such effect to a simple story by the form in which it is expressed—at least in conversation, for the expression is ill suited to written prose style. For example, telling how a horseman rode past without stopping, a Turk said to me, " He came, he passed, he went " (*geldi, getchdi, gitdi*). If he calls to a man to bring water, he says, " Water take, come " (*su al gel*). In June, 1883, I was told of a village with "marbles in it" an hour to the west away off the road. A sudden thunderstorm came on: our way lay across fields, which after ten minutes' downpour became seas of liquid mud, intersected by several watercourses, deep ditches with steep sides five to ten feet high, down which the horses slid, and up which they contrived to scramble in some mysterious way after several vain attempts and with many slips. We got through without mishap, strange to say, taking an hour and a half to do an easy hour's distance. The village was a miserable set of four or five small houses ; in the wall of one was a scrap of marble. As we circled round the last house, my man said, " We have come, we have seen, there is not " (*geldik, geurduk, yok*) ; and we silently turned to the north.

It is only the elderly men whom one meets in the Oda ; and undoubtedly, part of the reason why the villagers impress one so favourably is that there are so few young men at home. A group of young rustics, loutish, awkward, ignorant, rude, is a spectacle that you rarely see ; but some examples come before you of the horseplay, coarse and even filthy in character, which furnishes their amusement. The squads of recruits whom one occasionally meets are capable of much harm, an example of which is given on p. 205. From what I have in some rare cases seen, and from what I have heard on unimpeachable authority, it is clear how much is gained from the absence of the young men in most cases. The requirements of military service take many away. Others are sent by their family to some of the great cities, where a little money can be earned by serving as porters or in some other humble employment : at home, of course, there is no possible way by which a halfpenny could be earned by the utmost industry, for nobody wants any work done, and nobody posesses any money to pay for work, if he wanted it.

Coined money, even in the smallest quantities, simply does not exist in villages. At first I could not realise it in spite of warnings, and was disposed at times to think that the villagers were trying to extort a dollar on the plea of having no change. But that idea cannot last in the face of what occurs; for example, you find a man ready to walk beside your party an hour's journey in order to get the change (to his own disadvantage) at a market town where a shop exists. There are no shops, no circulation of money, no possibility of exchanging the fruits of labour for pleasures, or luxuries, or any variety from the simplest and barest necessities of life. This may seem an idyllic style of life to some social theorists; but I should be glad to make them travel continuously for three years among Turkish villages, so that they may realise what the want of sale implies. The shop cannot exist because there is no money to buy from it, and no security for earnings if money could be got ; robbery is indeed rare in the villages at present, because there is absolutely nothing to steal ; but few men would care to be known as the only person in a village that possessed some money and articles for sale. Moreover, if the shopkeeper escaped open robbery, he would be a prey to the extortionate demands of every zaptieh (policeman). No one tries to earn : there is nothing to earn, and, if he could earn anything, the zaptiehs would hear of it and exact heavy toll on it.

The worst consequence of this want of work is the idleness and ignorance in which the men grow up. The women do all the field work, necessary to grow the year's supply of food ; the men lounge about in laziness or in mischief, until conscription calls them away, or family embarrassment drives them to Smyrna or some such place. Then their education commences : they begin to have the training of real, steady work, and often the vulgar and objectionable lout develops easily into a trustworthy and good man. Wherever any work has to be done for which absolute honesty is required, there it is always a Turk that is employed : they are the human watchdogs whom every one employs and trusts. If you sent any ordinary poor Turk, picked up by accident, to carry £100 to some place, it is wonderful in how many cases it would be delivered safely and intact by a man to whom £5 represents a fortune; and not merely would he carry it safe, but he would as a rule defend it, if attacked, and fight till he dropped.

Nothing is ever repaired in Turkey. A building once made is allowed to stand until it becomes uninhabitable. In the better houses, the ground floor is used for stables and lumber-room, and the dwelling rooms are all on the upper floor. If one of the steps in the wooden ladder or staircase that leads to the dwelling-rooms is broken, you must make a greater effort at that point, such is the will of God: so long as it is possible to ascend, things will be left untouched. Apparently, when a house decays, it is preferred to build a new one elsewhere. Hence the traveller is often struck by the number of ruined hovels, through which he has to pass before reaching the inhabited part of a town. Konia, for example, seems to be a city of the dead, if you enter it from some directions, for you ride through streets of roofless, empty, mud-brick houses. The author of *Anadol* speaks at Kaisari about " the neglected aspect ; great khans are deserted and crumbling to ruins, warehouses empty, bazaars only half occupied, and not a street without its rows of uninhabited houses, and many gaps where houses had fallen altogether . . . all displayed a depressed and languishing appearance, as if life were fast waning from Cæsarea ". In 1890 the parts of Kaisari which I saw were much better : the development of Armenian activity in recent years had caused a general renovation.

Thus almost everything in Turkey, whether public or private property, with few exceptions (and those usually directed by Europeans), goes surely to ruin.

Akhmet, a Koniali (from a village, eleven hours west of Konia), who was one of our men in 1886, had served seven years as a soldier, had risen to the rank of sergeant, had gone through the earlier stages of the Russian war, and the siege of Plevna ; he had been taken prisoner when Plevna was captured (one of 140 men who survived out of a regiment 700 strong), and had been released at the end of the war. During his seven years of service, he had received one dollar as pay. He was an excellent specimen of a village Turk : absolutely trustworthy, strong, slow, steady, modest, quiet, perfectly well-behaved, and perfectly useless in all the departments of work where any skill or readiness was required. When he came to a village, instead of putting on some show and making an impression of importance, he would take the humblest inhabitant aside and inquire in a whisper where he could procure milk, a fowl, etc. He never knew what to do or to say beyond his ordinary round of duties; he could never learn to distinguish between a stone without letters and a " written stone "; he never could see why I looked at such things, and much as he tried, never could feel the faintest interest in them (even though he knew *bakshish* rewarded every discovery).

But the Turks are not by any means absolutely uniform in character. In 1884 we had a man from a village east of Kaisari in Cappadocia. His name was Omar; and he usually answered to the name of Hadji. But his pilgrimage had not been to Mecca; he had merely visited some Armenian sacred place, which I forget; and that in itself is a remarkable fact. There is a certain awe attached even among the Moslem peasantry to the old holy places of the Christians;[1] and they believe that some supernatural power resides in them, and some merit is gained by visiting them. Such a belief is quite generally recognised as regards Jerusalem, and many Turks have mentioned it to me; but, as regards other places, the respect felt seems to be merely a local superstition, which would not be generally approved.

Hadji Omar was the ablest and most useful man whom I ever had with me. He was moderately

[1] Chapter xi.

tall, about 5 ft. 11 in., fair of hair and complexion, quick at picking up new ideas and methods, adapting himself easily to new circumstances. He thoroughly recognised that his business was to find inscriptions; and he literally left no stone unturned. Everything he was told to do was done well; and he showed himself in a great variety of characters during our four and a half months' travelling, ending up with a public sale of horses, in which he proved a most skilful auctioneer. He possessed that character which English people, when they see it in other nations, stigmatise as grasping, but which in themselves they consider as a proper regard for their own interest. The Hadji had his way to make in the world; the connection with us gave him his first chance in life, and he was resolved to use it. He realised from his service a number of pounds, which would enable him to retire to his own country and live as a man of wealth for the future. Money which once touched his palm never left it except to enter the folds of his girdle; but he was strict in his accounts; and if he exacted a full toll for all that he did—as for example the auctioneer's percentage on the selling-price of every horse—it was done in a strictly business way; and I have never had such pleasure in giving any man his baksheesh, as I had in giving him quadruple my usual amount. He never shirked any work imposed on him, and he never grumbled at any fatigue. That it was all done from regard for his own ultimate advantage is doubtless true; but it was an enlightened self-interest that ruled his action. If a flower could be found within a mile of the camp, he had a nosegay ready for my wife every morning.

He had undoubtedly in him the capacity for cruelty; and it would go hard with any man who stood between him and his advantage. He seemed to me to have about him far more of the European than of the Asiatic character. I have always suspected him of being a Kurd, rather than a Turk; and another man whom I had with me and who hated the Hadji with a desperate hatred, a Turk from Bosnia and a good man himself, always declared that Omar was no Turk and a sham Hadji. Good luck to the Hadji; and when next I travel, may I find another like him.

Yet, if I ever come to be in a really dangerous situation, it would be the rather stupid but absolutely honest Koniali, and not the much abler Kaisarli, that I should wish to have beside me—if I could not have both. There lies the reason why I have always such affection for the Turkish villager. A nation, to be great and self-sufficient, must consist of more than faithful watchdogs; but those who have known the need of them will never undervalue the watchdogs.

But the two examples I have selected are better by far than the average. To make the balance more even, let me add that the most repulsive and detestable of all the men I ever had about me was a mulatto Turk, of huge bulk and hideous face, utterly untrustworthy, lazy, and useless, not wholly stupid, but so incapable of honest service that his work never could be good.

In one respect a strong contrast between the average Turkish and Greek villages impressed me. In Turkish villages the women, so far as I can judge from sight and report, are feebler and poorer in both physique and mind (owing to their hard lot in childhood); whereas the Greek women struck me as being better and morally higher than the men, physically good and intellectually well developed. Therein lies the future of the two races. In the one case you have a rich soil from which future generations acquire strength and moral vigour ; in the other a stunted and impoverished motherhood produces a poor and diminishing people. In the condition of the Turkish women lies the reason for the steady degeneration of the Turkish people.

CHAPTER III.

THE best way of showing how the accidents of travel and the character of the Turks and Turkmens come before the traveller is to describe a single excursion, and attempt to bring out a few of the varied thoughts that rise in one's mind amid the scenery and the men that one is thrown among. As this requires a certain breadth of treatment, I select the shortest excursion that I ever made, when, owing to engagements at home, I had at the utmost only twenty days at my disposal to go from and return to Smyrna. In many ways it was the least productive and the most fatiguing excursion that I was ever engaged in, because a long distance had to be traversed in a very short time, and if you want to make discoveries you must be prepared to apply patience and leisure, and to spend days where on this occasion I spent hours. For clearness' sake the narrative is numbered as a diary.

I. In July, 1888, a short excursion was needed to verify a report about an undiscovered monument in Northern Phrygia. Before starting from the railway terminus at Serai-Keui I went to Smyrna for a day, to see my wife off in the Messageries steamer, leaving my men to await my return. On the third day, when the train arrived, two Turkish servants with three horses were standing ready. We got off at once, and rode away over the valley, crossing the narrow Lycos river, a muddy and apparently deep stream, flowing between steep banks about ten feet high or more, like a big ditch. It is easily bridged, even by Turks, with a few pine trunks and cross planks ; but, narrow though it be, it is quite unfordable. The Crusaders under King Louis could ford the broad Mæander, not far away ; but I doubt if they could have crossed the Lycos, insignificant though it be, without a bridge ; those steep high banks, and the soft mud of the channel, seem a hopeless obstacle.

It is difficult, and it would be unfair to a most " gallant feat of arms," to go across the Mæander or Lycos valley without thinking of that New Year's Day in 1148, when the French army[1] had the deep Mæander in front of them, with a Turkish army drawn up on the opposite bank. The Mæan-

[1] Nicetas describes this brilliant action as performed by Conrad and his army ; in that case the crossing would have been in the Lycos valley. But he is wrong (see my *Cities and Bishoprics of Phrygia*, p. 162), having confused the two allied armies. Conrad turned back before reaching the Mæander. Louis crossed lower down the river.

der, difficult to cross at any time, was believed to be quite unfordable at that season ; there were no boats, and the bridge had been destroyed. But Louis himself set the example, and his army marched down into the stream, across it, up the other bank, and over or through the opposing Turks.

It is three hours' ride across the Lycos valley to where the steep ascent begins up the mountains on the northern side. On the outer fringe lies Hierapolis with its white cascade of rocks shining in the sun, about six miles to the right of the point where we began to ascend. After an hour's climb we reached a little village beside the path, where my other servant was expecting us. His orders had been to start from Serai-Keui in the forenoon, and have everything ready for us when we arrived between eight and nine o'clock at night. He had charge of one baggage horse, while he rode the horse which until three days ago had been used by Mrs. Ramsay. I wanted to make a very rapid journey, and kept all equipment as light as possible, so that we had still exactly the same number of horses and servants, as when she was with us. But it is one thing to give orders in Turkey, and a very different thing to have them executed when you are far away. We found our man (who in many respects was an unusually active and useful Turk) sitting among the villagers; nothing had been unpacked, no preparations made, no fowl purchased. As he explained, there had not been time to do anything when he saw us coming across the valley; and he waited to see whether I still wanted him to carry out the orders. At that hour it was too late to prepare anything; sardines and tea, the usual stand-by on a late arrival, furnished a hurried meal.

Our quarters were very picturesque. A small platform of rough planks was fixed under the shadow of two overarching trees; and the hillside was so steep that from the outer edge of the platform there was a drop of some hundred feet. Round the platform ran a low balustrade. Here the village men usually sat in the cool shade with a splendid outlook across the plain to the southern mountains, where Kadmos and Salbakos, both still crowned with snow, stood up from the valley (550 feet above sea level in the middle) to a height of over 8000 feet. The change from the heat and dust of Smyrna and the railway carriage and the valley, to this rustic seat on the side of the hill, was delightful.

II. Early in the morning we reached the summit of the hills that bound the Lycos valley. The muleteer was sent on from here to Demirji-Keui (where the whole district Tchal used to go for a blacksmith, *demirji*). He had strict orders to be better prepared this evening ; and I made sure that he bought a fowl before we left the village. The rest of us were to visit various villages, and to reach Demirji-Keui in the evening. At this point we were supposed to be half-way between Serai-Keui and Demirji-Keui, six hours from each.

At this point the traveller appreciates the true character of the Lycos valley. He stands here on the rim of that great plateau, 3000 to 5000 feet in height, which forms the main mass of Asia Minor, and from which protrude, like fingers stretched to the west, mountain chains reaching to the Ægean Sea, and often extending far out as narrow peninsulas into the sea. He sees that the glen of the Lycos is a deep hole in the side of this plateau, sloping upwards and eastwards as it narrows, like a funnel leading up to the level of the plateau. North of it and south of it the plateau sweeps onward to the west.

The great plateau is bordered all round by an irregular rim of mountains, like the sides of a billiard-table, broken only by occasional narrow gorges, through which rivers force their passage into the low coast valleys. Where we ascended, the rim is about 4000 feet high ; and from it we have an extensive view to the north over the plateau. This part of the plateau is a great plain called Banaz-Ova, about thirty-five miles by twenty-five, over which lies our journey for some days. You look across it to Mount Dindymos on the north, and Burgas Dagh on the east; and, as you look from here, the plain seems flat and riverless and treeless. But when you travel across it, you find that it is intersected by great cañons. The streams which come down into the plain, flow at first near its level; but gradually their channels grow deeper, as they converge towards the south-west, until they become cañons with almost perpendicular sides, 200, 500, 1000 feet in height. At last all the cañons are merged in that of the Mæander, which breaks through the mountain rim at the south-west corner into the Lycos valley in a gorge of wonderful grandeur and beauty, well worth a tourist's journey.

The broken country in the southern part of the Banaz-Ova, near the Mæander, is the rich and fertile district of Tchal, in which we were to spend the next twenty-four hours.

At lunch that day, in a village Ak-Dere-Devrent (Guardhouse on the White Gorge), I was told that some stones, covered with figures and writing, had recently been found in a field below Geuzlar (the Arches). I listened almost with sorrow, for Demirji-Keui was four hours to the east and Geuzlar three hours to the west of us; when I heard of the stones it was already past two o'clock; reports of this kind in many cases turn out to be false or exaggerated; and I was hurrying towards the north. But a man, whose conversation showed quite unusual knowledge for a Turk, assured me that these stones were remarkable; and I could not pass them by. One of my men was sent off to Demirji-Keui; if I did not appear there in the evening, the muleteer and he were instructed to meet us on the following evening at Duman, a village about six hours north from Demirji-Keui; the other man and I went off to the "Arches". The track was bad, winding in some places along the edge of steep ravines, and could not safely be traversed in the dark. At the village I found a man to take me to the stones, which lay in a field, a mile beyond: they were two huge slabs of marble, containing rude reliefs of a religious character, and lists of subscribers, all with their portraits; a point in topography, hitherto controverted and obscure, was illuminated by the inscriptions, and I felt rewarded. Had there been more time, I should have made drawings; but that would have required most of the next day, and in my hurry the stones seemed not to deserve such honour. In their position they could not be photographed, even if I had had a camera.

The sun's rays were still touching the top of the

walls of the huge gorge, breaking down towards the Mæander, at the head of which stands Geuzlar, as we left the stones, and climbed up the steep ascent to the village, where my man waited with our horses. As it was impossible to reach camp that night, he had been ordered to find quarters in the village, buy whatever could be got, and prepare dinner.

The village occupies an extraordinarily secluded and retired position, considering how near it is to the railway and the great trade-route, which runs through the Lycos valley on its way from the far East to the Ægean Sea. Owing to the interruption of communication by the great cañon of the Mæander, which breaks through the mountains a little to the west, Geuzlar lies at its world's end, and you cannot take it on the way to anywhere else ; to reach it the traveller must turn his back on the rest of the world, and to leave it he must go back the way he came (unless he descends its gorge into the cañon of the Mæander, and then finds his way out of that, which is possible for one who loves to go, where no one else ever goes, by a path of singular grandeur). In this remote position, so unknown that I did not learn of its existence until 1888, Geuzlar became the refuge of a remnant of some old population, which has been exterminated elsewhere. Its people would be a study for an ethnologist ; and I hope that Dr. Von Luschan, who has devoted such care and skill to the study of the Lycian peoples, will visit it. They are small in stature ; I saw no one who seemed over about five feet four ; whereas, in general, the Turks of Anatolia, especially those of the mountains, are a big, powerful race. They are also peculiarly ugly in face, which is far from being the case with the Turks ; and yet there was a 'certain good-natured look about them. One almost unique fact was that in this rather large village, they declared there was no guest-house (*Musafir-Oda*). My man met me with this news ; as he could find no house, he had thought it unnecessary to look after food ; but he had put the horses in a stable.

When I insisted that there must be some place where strangers could spend the night, they conducted us to a low lean-to shanty, beside a midden, with a door through which a large-sized dog could have just entered without stooping, a shanty in which no decent person would have housed a dog ; and gravely proposed that we should spend the night there. My Turk was in despair, and seemed inclined to make the best of this kennel. Luckily, as we came along I had observed a fine airy verandah in front of a good house ; and I explained to them that I was going to spend the night in that verandah, and would pay for the accommodation. They were not very willing, and my man after some whispering said to me that it was impossible, for there was a woman in the house. But, as no woman could be seen from outside, I went up the ladder stairs, telling the man to make a bargain. Had there been a woman in sight, it would have been rudeness to insist ; but, so long as no signs of one were visible, I was within a guest's right to accommodation. Meanwhile I sat down on the floor of the verandah to wait till things arranged themselves, as they always do in Turkey if you are clear about what you want. What became of the woman inside the house I did not learn ; but I was resolved not to quit the verandah, except to go to an inhabitable place. The negotiations took some time ; so we again dined off sardines and tea, but had to be content with unleavened bread from the village in place of the supply of good bread from Serai-Keui, which had gone on with the pack horse.

Another unusual characteristic of this village was that no one came to speak to us or look at us that evening or the next morning. Only the owner came for his rent (about two shillings). That is the only village in Turkey where I spent a night without hearing a word of welcome or of farewell.

In several other villages of Tchal, the people seemed to me ruder than ordinary Turks ; and racial difference is undoubtedly the reason.

III. On this day we went four hours eastwards over country broken by deep gorges, down which in time of rain torrents run north to the Mæander ; and then turned towards north-east, and at last north, through various villages, wondering as we rode whether the other men would understand the instructions, and also whether the Kaimmakam would allow them to obey. We crossed the cañon of the Mæander, at a point where the river is about 1600 feet above sea level ; and soon after heard at a village that our men had passed on their way to Duman, two hours further north. Duman was once perhaps the Phrygian village Tymion, where the Montanists pitched their " New Jerusalem," calling on all true Christians to come out from among the nations and dwell apart. It lies among hills, full 3500 feet above the sea, in a glen sloping down to the east ; and among its semi-nomadic people, with flocks all around, we found, as always among nomads (except some Kurds), a most hospitable welcome.

IV. From Duman we descended the glen to the open level stretch of the Banaz-Ova, and for two days rode north by east over the plain, choosing a line untraversed before, which proved unremunerative, and touched hardly any villages. Early on the first day we went through the site of Justinianopolis, which was founded by Justinian, after he had destroyed with fire and sword the remnants of the old Montanist sect and their city Pepouza. A line a little further east would have touched more villages, where remains brought from the three old cities that formerly stood on the east edge of Banaz-Ova might be expected ; but wisdom came too late. One valueless inscription was found in a village where we spent the night.

V. On the fifth day at noon we reached the site of Keramon-Agora, at the north-east corner of Banaz-Ova, that "great and peopled city" where Xenophon and the Ten Thousand spent a night. I recopied and greatly improved the text of the difficult inscription in which a third century Christian gave a small piece of ground to his church in its legally organised form as a benefit and burial society, with provision for workmen to keep it in order, on condition that the grave of his wife should be kept blooming with roses ; and found several unimportant stones which had escaped us in 1881 and 1883. Of the ancient city nothing remains visible above ground except scattered stones. Part of the afternoon was given to a little excursion to two villages a few miles to the west, which I had on former occasions passed by unvisited ; but this produced only six insignificant epitaphs.

VI. This forenoon, our road lay up one of the great passes of history, or rather a pass never actually mentioned in history, but great in actual fact. A number of roads from the west and south meet near Keramon-Agora, ascend the glen down which Hammam-Su (Bath-River) flows into Banaz-Ova, and diverge towards north and east on the high ground above the sources of that river. Although my aim had always been to try new routes every journey, yet this was the eighth time I had gone up or down that pass ; and here, in the first village we came to after leaving Keramon-Agora, I made the best find of this journey, and one of the most important that has ever fallen to my lot. Having often been in this village, I did not intend to stop there ; but, as we rode through, we halted for a moment to speak to a native who recognised me from of old. He told us of a new " written stone " ; and we dismounted and went under his charge to a good house, with a verandah, one of whose supporting columns rested on the inscribed face of an ancient marble, concealing great part of the letters. Enough, however, remained to show the general drift and most of the important details of the text. It was an inscription erected by the synagogue in honour of a woman, Julia Severa, who had built a new place of worship for them. In itself it seems, and is, a poor thing, but in the proper point of view it reveals to us a singularly important and interesting chapter of history.

In the third and second centuries B.C., many thousands of families of Jews from Babylonia were settled as colonists in the cities, which the Seleucid kings built or re-organised to be loyal garrisons and centres of the new civilising influence, in this alien and barbarian land of Phrygia. These Jews are often referred to in the Talmud, which complains that " the baths and wines of Phrygia had separated the Ten Tribes from their brethren ". We know from the Book of Acts that they had great influence in such Phrygian cities as Antioch and Iconium, and we learn from Cicero that their numbers in his time were very great. All modern experience suggests that a Jewish population like this must have exercised a profound influence on the development of the country. Further, there was also a considerable Jewish population in the chief Italian cities, and in several other parts of the Roman empire. The question suggests itself, whether there was a Jewish aristocracy in the Roman world. The attempt to answer that question was made almost hopeless by the fact that these Jews adopted Greek or Roman names and manners ; and were therefore undistinguishable from Greeks and Romans in the superficial view which alone was permitted us in the dearth of evidence.

The foundations of an answer to this question, so far as concerns Phrygia, are laid by this inscription. Julia Severa, who is mentioned in it as a leader and benefactor among the Jewish people, is named frequently on coins of Akmonia. In no other case is any single individual mentioned so often on the coins of any city in the country. If she was a Jewess, the Jews must have enjoyed great influence and honour in Akmonia; and from this beginning we are led on through a series of identifications to the theory of Jewish power in Phrygia, which is stated in my chapter on " The Jews in Phrygia ".[1] I have been told that a distinguished German scholar has found a new inscription throwing much additional and corroborative light on the subject.

Late in the afternoon we reached a considerable village, where I felt much inclined to halt for the night; but as it wanted still a full hour to sunset, and a village Hamil-Keui was reported an hour ahead, we very unwillingly rode on, leaving one of the men to make sure that the muleteer, who was some distance behind, should come on to Hamil-Keui. We had to cross a ridge of bare hills, of no

---

[1] *Cities and Bishoprics of Phrygia*, ch. xv.

great height; a thunderstorm came on when we were near the top, and in the heavy rain we lost the sense of direction, and wandered away to the east, instead of keeping north-east. We struck a river, which, as I knew, flowed in the direction we were going; but the existing maps did not show that here it makes a great loop, flowing round two-thirds of a circle. We went round with it, and at last saw a village half a mile up from the stream. Despairing of ever reaching Hamil-Keui, we went to this village, and found that we were at Hamil-Keui, and that our packs had arrived an hour ago. I had never made such an egregious error, or so entirely lost the estimate of locality, since 1881, when after sunset on a late November evening we found ourselves wandering over the Banaz-Ova in search of Suleimanli, without any idea whether it lay west or south or north.

Hamil-Keui was a fair specimen of the Turkish *tchiftlik* village, where the land is not village property, but is in private hands. As a general rule, when, on entering a village, you are struck with the appearance of extreme dilapidation, discomfort and wretchedness, the houses being mere small huts of the poorest, lowest and most sordid type, constructed apparently of little except mud and thatch, you will be told, if you ask the question, that this is a *tchiftlik*. There are exceptions, not merely those

which belong to Christians, like that described on
p. 132, but occasionally on estates owned by Turks.
At Buldur, a large town on Lake Askania, I met a
very intelligent young Turk in 1884, who had some
education, spoke a little French, was the son of a
once well-known Pasha of liberal tendencies, and held
some official position in a sort of honorary banish-
ment from Constantinople. He told me of ruins
on his estate, six hours to the south ; and on his
invitation I went there for a day, and was struck
with the air of activity, and the higher standard of
comfort and equipment, pervading the establishment.

But, as a rule, the *tchiftliks* owned by Turks are
of a very different character (except in the case of
the old-fashioned proprietors who live on their own
estate among their tenants). The people cultivate
the soil on the *métayer* system, their houses are
given them by the lord of the manor, and everything and every person wears an air of depression
and squalor. This statement, which results from
years of observation in Asia Minor, agrees exactly
with what an authority of far greater experience,
" A Consul's Daughter and Wife," says about the
tchiftliks of Macedonia ;[1] there is only this difference
that in Macedonia " the tenants are with few exceptions Christians," in Asia Minor they are Turks
(so far as my experience goes).

[1] See *The People of Turkey*, i., p. 205 ff.

There was no guest-house in Hamil-Keui. Seeing the hovel in front of which the muleteer was standing, little better than the kennel in which the people of Geuzlar had proposed to put us, I asked with horror if this were the Oda: the whole concourse replied that here there was not a village but a *tchiftlik*, obviously implying that such a luxury as an Oda could not exist on a *tchiftlik*. On a fine night I would have camped out rather than enter that squalid hole, where there was hardly room to turn and just room to stand upright ; but rain was still heavy, and shelter was absolutely necessary. I insisted on seeing some other houses ; but all were the same ; and there was nothing for it but to be content with Hamil-Keui, and learn by practical experience the difference between land cultivated for the benefit of a landlord, and land cultivated for the benefit of the cultivators.

VII. This day we went by a picturesque road down the river. This is the main stream of the Tembris or Tembrogius, called lower down Porsuk-Su, from a *tchiftlik* in a remarkable situation on the river bank, where it issues from a mountain-gorge a little above Kutaya. Porsuk is an old Turkish personal name, grecized by Anna Comnena as Prosoukhos ; but all the map-drawers and travellers call the river Pursak or Pursek. Two hours below Hamil-Keui the Tembris issues from the hills into a great valley, once inhabited by the people Praipenisseis. As it issues out of its narrow glen it flows past a large tumulus, round which is a village called Besh-Karish-Eyuk (Five-Span-Mound). A legend which I omitted to note down is connected with this mound. So far as I was able to judge, folk tales are poor and uninteresting among the Turks; but it requires wider knowledge and greater freedom in the Turkish language than I possess to gather the materials for a correct judgment on this subject.

One and a half hours across the plain brought us to Altun-Tash (Gold-Stone), chief village of the district, and half-way halting place between Kutaya and Afiom-Kara-Hissar. It is full of inscriptions, most of which are disappointing. Here we spent two hours about noon. In the afternoon, at a village Tchakirsaz, one hour to the east of Altuntash, inscriptions detained us some time. One was the quarry mark on a block of Synnadic marble, showing that the marble of those quarries was not merely carried to Rome, but also sold in other directions. The others were unimportant and difficult epitaphs, one of which had some turns of expression, suggesting Christian origin; but in its fragmentary condition, certainty was impossible. This great valley was one of the chief centres of Christianity in Phrygia during the third century;

and a considerable number of Christian epitaphs are found in it.

After leaving Tchakirsaz, we crossed the line of the new road leading direct from Kutaya to Afiom-Kara-Hissar. Though occasionally one finds a good new road, built by some European in the government service, the great majority of the roads which have been made in recent years in Asia Minor are bad. In more cases than one, the line of the new road was indicated to our eyes by the deeper green of a more luxuriant crop of grass ; the natives carefully avoided it, because its surface was not so good for horses' feet ; and the track which they followed kept away from the road, only cutting across it occasionally. It is quite common to find an isolated piece of modern road without beginning or end. It is still commoner to find an elevated causeway, built at great expense, leading to the bank of a ravine or stream, in preparation for a bridge ; but the bridge has never been built, and, if you are not looking ahead, you are discomposed by your horse coming to a sudden halt, with his fore legs planted firm, refusing to make the next step, which would precipitate him into the yawning chasm. When a new road is projected, an entirely new line is selected, often one that requires engineering works of some magnitude : scraps of the road are made by forced labour : a certain amount of money is spent : three times as much money is 'embezzled by officials of various ranks : then the whole enterprise is abandoned. If, instead of these ambitious projects, one quarter of the labour were expended on the existing routes, bridging and improving the worst parts, far more good would be done ; but, then, officials could not make so much money.

Two hours towards the east, along a hill-path crossing a succession of water-courses which ran down from a bald range of hills on our left, brought us to Kadi-Musal, a village lying on the sloping hillside about 3700 feet above sea-level, and commanding a very extensive view to the south. The day had been chilly after the thunderstorm of yesterday, and in the late afternoon showers of rain fell : very unusual weather for this season.

VIII. This morning a ride of an hour and a half brought us to Duwer (the Wall), from which my quest was to start. In the summer of 1887, returning towards Smyrna across the Banaz-Ova, I got into conversation one day with a man who told me that he belonged to Duwer, and that there was a wonderful monument close to a small Turbe (Mohammedan shrine), about an hour on the other side of the village. I have always thought, and believe to the present day, that there remain some Phrygian monuments to be discovered in the country that lies north and north-east from Duwer; this account seemed to confirm my view, and my special object in this hurried run was to verify the report, and discover the wonderful monument. At Duwer we found a guide to the Turbe, left our packs in quarters for the night, and went away in eager expectation. To my dismay the guide turned to the south; and after about an hour we reached the Turbe, and found that it was close to the splendid monument Arslan-Kaya (Lion Rock) which Sterrett and I had found in 1883, and published in the *Journal of Hellenic Studies*, 1884. At that time I had not learned how important it is to notice such signs of Mohammedan beliefs as a Turbe; and had passed by the small modern building with contempt. Now that I have learned better, I should inquire the name of the Dede who is buried or supposed to be buried there, and ask about the foundation legend connected with it. But it was only in 1891 that I began to realise how the awe attaching to old sites and old centres of religion or superstition has perpetuated itself among the Turks in the form of the Dede, whose grave is shown as a holy place, sometimes possessing miraculous powers. Had I inquired in 1883 about the Dede and Turbe near Arslan-Kaya, I should have been spared the hurried excursion whose fortunes are here set forth; but also I should have missed the discovery of

Julia Severa's inscription, and of the Jewish families connected with her.

This was one of my greatest disappointments, for the report had been so circumstantial and so probable, that I had never doubted about some great find ; and the man had been right in every respect except one ; he had described the monument as north or north-east of the village, whereas it lay to the south. The day, too, was cold and showery : when the sun is bright, disappointments are light, but I find them much harder to bear, when I am cold and the sky is dark.

There was now no other course open than to return to Duwer and try to get better news there. But we could not hear of any other monument, whether because the Duwerli knew of none, or because I failed to make them talk. In my dejection I was not in the humour to get on well with the usual crowd of natives, and in such circumstances they were not likely to tell much. As the rain came heavier, it did not seem advisable to pack up and go on, so I contented myself with riding an hour north over the watershed to make the connection with a former route, and then came back to bed feeling despondent. Rainy weather is peculiarly depressing on these expeditions, for there is absolutely nothing to do except work ; and when you are confined inside a hut, archæologising seems a cold and hollow occupation. This was our first blank day.

IX. The distance to Afiom-Kara-Hissar (Opium-Black-Castle) from Duwer is called ten hours; but with our faces turned to the south and towards home we did it without feeling any temptation to halt, for the same cold, bleak, showery weather continued in a way I have never known here in July. I knew every foot of the way and of the country immediately around, while the unpropitious weather did not tempt us to search for fresh woods and pasture new.

Afiom-Kara-Hissar, with its citadel high on a vast, almost inaccessible column of rock rising straight out of the plain to a height of 700 feet,[1] was a point of great importance in the long wars between Christian and Mohammedan. In 668, the Arabs besieged Constantinople, only forty-six years after Mohammed fled, helpless and almost alone, from Mecca. But in 740, in front of the walls of Akroênos, a Byzantine army won the first victory over the Crescent, the victory that cheered on the Romaic soldiers to the long wars of the following

[1] 800 Sir C. Wilson; 626 Monsieur G. Radet.

two centuries, in which step by step they rolled back the tide of Mohammedanism, and extended the Byzantine Empire further to the east than the Roman Empire in its palmiest days. Akroênos is the Turkish Afiom-Kara-Hissar. The great fortress, called also Nikopolis, the City of Victory, inherited the people and the marbles of the old Phrygian city, Prymnessos, three miles distant south by east, through the centre of which our journey lies to-morrow.

Afiom-Kara-Hissar is one of the rainiest places that I know : perhaps the lofty mountains close on the south catch the rain-clouds drifting south from the Black Sea. But, whatever be the reason, it has rained almost every time I have been at Kara-Hissar ; I should except November, 1881, when it only snowed. The town was true to its character ; and this afternoon had to be spent in a khan under shelter. In another respect I had better luck. The officials made no difficulties : generally I have had to make two or three visits to the Konak at this city, and go through a lot of trouble.

This was again a blank day.

X. Six hours through a country full of interest, where I ought to have spent at least two long days, brought us to Tchifut-Kassaba (Jews-Market), the site of Synnada, which lies almost due south of Kara-Hissar. The cold continued, but no rain fell.

The afternoon was spent looking for new inscriptions; a few new things had turned up since my last visit, but nothing of importance rewarded our efforts. Synnada lies high, about 3700 feet, under the lofty ridge of volcanic mountains that stretch south from Kara-Hissar, at the west end of a fine fertile valley, which stretches out before the city for seven or eight miles (exactly as Strabo describes it).

Turkish towns are generally placed where a copious supply of running water is available with little trouble. In some large towns, the water flows continuously through most of the streets ; and in almost all there is abundance of fountains running constantly. The ancient cities, on the other hand, were placed rather with a view either to convenience of trade or to military strength ; and, as there was far greater engineering skill among the ancients, they did not shrink from the task of conducting an artificial water-supply to their cities from a considerable distance. Tchifut-Kassaba seems, however, to stand actually on part of the site of Synnada ; and the acropolis of the ancient city is at the edge of the modern. There are numerous fountains, which pour an abundant supply of water through the town. The water is brought in underground channels from the hills near the city on the west side. There are Greek workmen in Turkey who still possess some considerable skill in making such underground channels for water. I once saw one of these workmen engaged in arranging the water-supply for a village in Banaz-Ova : he had nearly finished the work, but as it was still incomplete I had the opportunity of seeing great part of the aqueduct. It was apparently an old channel, which had been broken ; and until the repairs were completed the village had to carry all its water from the break, about half a mile away, while the new fountain in which the aqueduct was to end, was as yet quite dry.

XI. From Synnada to Tatarli, at the north-east end of the long valley called in ancient times Metropolitanus Campus, and now Turkmen-Ova or Tchul-Ova,[1] is six hours due south by the horse road over the hills, and eight hours by the araba road. As we had traversed in 1881 the easy road round the eastern end of the rough ridge, which, stretching out from the lofty volcanic mountains west of Synnada, separates the Synnada valley from that of Metropolis, I determined this time to take the horse road.

Our road led through or near a series of villages, almost all of which contain numerous traces of ancient life. Most of these villages I had visited in October, 1881 ; and on this occasion I did not find any new inscription, till we entered a glen that

---

[1] The shape of the valley suggested the name tchul (sack).

ascended towards the south, where a stone in a fountain bore an interesting epigram. About six miles south of Synnada we reached a village Baghche-Hissar (Garden-Castle, incorrectly in maps Baljik-Hissar), near the top of the glen. Here the villagers told us that a conical hill above the village on the east contained many traces of *Djineviz* (old walls), but that there were no inscribed stones there. Then a villager told us that he knew of a stone among the hills with letters on it; but it was not marble, only " black stone ". He said it was two hours distant, close to our road ; and I induced him to come and show it, by promising him a good reward, if it bore an inscription ; but payment was to be strictly by results ; no letters, no money. I was eager to get this inscription, as from his description, it seemed likely to be a boundary stone, and therefore perhaps of the highest importance and rarity. As these Turkish villagers are fickle and changeable, it is always advisable to go with them the moment they show any willingness : if you postpone for even a short time after they have been brought to the scratch, you are liable to find that their habitual sluggishness has resumed its sway, and it is doubly difficult, sometimes impossible, to get them started again.

We therefore sacrificed the *Djineviz* of the hill-city. It is remarkable how the name *Genoese* is applied to all ancient massive walls in Turkey; but this is perhaps due to the apparent connection with the Arabic Djin, the winged evil spirits, the *genii* of old-fashioned editions of the *Arabian Nights* and of *Tales of the Genii*. This name has caused some difficulty to travellers, who imagine that the Genoese must have been present wherever they find *Djineviz*. Hamilton refers to this idea in regard to the line of splendid khans from Trebizond to Tabriz:[1] "an opinion has gone abroad that they were erected by the Genoese when they possessed the trade of this country. To the Genoese are ascribed, also, the castles of Trebizond, Baiburt," etc. He proceeds to show that all these buildings are earlier in date than any Genoese settlements in Asia Minor.

Our road out of the village wound round the back of the *Djineviz* hill, and the fact was immediately plain that it had been cut out of the hillside with great care and skill. It led, with a steady, gradual ascent, round the south side of the hill, but was not intended as the access to a city on the top, for on the south-east side it turned away to the south, and wound in the same long curves and steady ascent up the pass towards Metropolis. It was obviously a Roman road leading southwards, for never has any race except the Romans ruled this country who undertook engineering works like

[1] *Researches in Asia Minor*, i., p. 185.

that; and it is the finest specimen of Roman road-engineering that I have seen in Asia Minor. Hitherto I had believed, and stated in print more than once as indubitable, that the Roman road from Synnada to Metropolis must have followed the longer line of the easy araba road, above described; but here was an obvious Roman road far up the pass, pointing towards Metropolis. About a mile or two on, our guide said the stone lay up the hillside to the west. I was eager to follow the Roman road as far as possible, and see whether it actually reached the summit of the pass; but, as there was good hope of returning again to the line of the road, which could be seen for some distance in front, I very unwillingly followed the Turk away to the right. He led us up among the hills higher and higher, further and further from the road, declaring always that the stone was quite close. At last near the highest part of the ridge, he declared that the stone was here, and, after hunting about for a minute, pointed out a rock on which were some natural marks, and claimed his reward. It was too aggravating! the Roman road was now hopelessly lost; the clouds had come down and rain was falling; everything seemed to be against us. It was clear that the man either had forgotten the exact spot where the inscribed stone was, or had got tired of the quest and wanted to get away home, for his description in no way corresponded to what he now showed us. I refused to pay him until he showed the lettered stone; and quoted the terms of the bargain. He argued that he had promised to show me a *kara-tash*, not a *mermer*; and this was a *kara-tash*. We all tried to show him that this argument was a fallacy; but he refused to be convinced; and his obstinate reiteration of this bad reasoning was not calculated to soothe our wounded feelings. I ordered him off, unless he showed us the "written stone"; and I shall never forget the look of misery that came over his face, as he realised that he was to get nothing. It has often haunted me since, by day and by night. I don't know how I was so stony hearted as to turn the poor fellow away, to walk back more than an hour in the rain without a penny; but at the moment I could not bear the loss of both the *Djineviz* and the Roman road. I still see the look that he cast back on me, as he turned slowly away, a ragged, bent, poverty-stricken old man of fifty, with his feet wrapt in old clouts in place of shoes, shuffling along in the regular Turkish style, having fallen from his golden dream to the hard reality of penury. A shilling to him would have made him contented and even rich: to me it was nothing; and yet I let him go away empty. It was an act

for which there can be no justification, no pallia-
tion. The letter of the bargain was on my side;
but the feeling that ought to rule in the conduct of
man to man condemns me absolutely. It is a
small incident in itself; but yet I doubt if anything in my whole life has cost me so much re-
morse. It was a typical example of the essential
immorality of rigorous legal right when exercised
by unsympathetic power.

We were in no pleasant situation ourselves; a
slight mist, accompanied by fine rain, contracted
the view on all sides; a sea of hills surrounded us;
it was near an hour since we had seen anything like
a path, and for the last half-hour we had been on
foot, as the ground was too rough to ride. In such
circumstances, one appreciates the value of a com-
pass. After we had dragged our horses behind us
for half an hour in the proper direction, the mist
lifted a little, and we saw far away in front the hills
dipping into the valley of Metropolis. There we
spent the evening without further misadventure and
without any new discovery.

Three years later, in 1891, when Mrs. Ramsay
and I crossed the higher mountains on the west, and
were coming down from the north-west side into the
valley of Metropolis, we heard of an inscription on
a *kara-tash*, beside the road from Metropolis to
Synnada. This time we were more lucky. We

found a boundary stone, letters roughly scratched on
a rock at the orders of an official, whose name also
occurs on two blocks of Synnadic marble which were
found in Rome : thus the three documents complete
each other, and prove that, in the reign of Trajan,
an imperial procurator at Synnada regulated the
boundaries between various tribes and cities of the
district, besides having the specifications inscribed
on blocks of marble for Rome under his responsibility.

It then became obvious that our guide in 1888
was seeking either for that boundary stone or for
another of the same series. Now the stone which
we found was full three hours distant from Baghche-
Hissar, whereas the guide turned away from the
road a bare hour from the village. Moreover the
guide expected to find his stone a long way from
the road among the hills, whereas the inscription
which we found was only about fifty yards from the
road on the brow of a bare slope leading down to
the valley of Metropolis. The guide, therefore,
must have been looking for a different boundary
stone from that which we found ; and the conclusion
is that it remains for some more fortunate or more
skilful traveller than I to find the reported inscription and probably to clear up the obscurities which
still envelop the topography of that district. He is
most likely to succeed, if he goes to the village

Alaka on the hills south of Baghche-Hissar, and contrives to find a guide there.[1]

XII. We crossed a steep and lofty mountain-ridge due south into the valley of Apollonia and Sozopolis (City of the Saviour), as the Christians called the Byzantine city on a lofty rock, which took the place of Apollonia when its situation in the open plain was found to be too unsafe. The day was spent in making a round of villages, verifying the text of published inscriptions, and, though tedious, it was profitable. In this southern valley we were plunged into the usual blazing heat of July; and the sudden change from the cold and rain of the past week was trying. At night I lay outside the stuffy Oda, with the horses too near; and the bad smell produced illness, as I have often experienced before.

XIII. Though hardly able to get on my horse, and frequently compelled to get off, I struggled on for an hour to Olu-Borlu, on the site of Sozopolis. After resting for an hour or two I went out in search of an important inscription, the published copy of which was unsatisfactory. According to my information it was in the courtyard of a *hodjire*, but when I asked for the *hodjire*, every one said that any place where a *hodja* lived was a *hodjire*. Taking a guide, I went about from place to place. Olu-

---

[1] *Cities and Bishoprics of Phrygia*, ch. xviii., and inscr. No. 693.

Borlu occupies two hills, with a valley between, and I was sent back and forward from one hill to the other, as each person who was consulted made some new suggestion. A growing crowd accompanied, until at last the whole male population of the town was perambulating from hill to hill and back again. I was still very ill, and was frequently obliged to halt, whereupon the whole crowd squatted or lounged about until I recovered, and was able to go on. In this way we trudged on, hour after hour, buoyed up by ever-renewed hopes, as somebody remembered some house that we had not seen which might correspond to the description, but always disappointed. One or two interesting things turned up, and at last sunset released me from torture. I had done my duty by that stone, and failed.

XIV. Seven hours to Apameia-Kelainai, now one of the termini of the Ottoman Railway, but in 1888 an insignificant village. At four hours from Olu-Borlu, we came to a stone, of which I was in search. I saw it in 1882, and read the name of the Emperor Hadrian at the beginning ; but as it was lying in a bad position I could not see the rest. I hoped now to find some means of moving the stone. Originally, the inscribed stone formed part of a monument, a great, tall, square pillar standing on a circular basis ; but the parts were now scattered, though apparently none were lost.

A man was sent on to the nearest village to hire workmen and bring a beam to use as a lever, and I sat down to wait. A few minutes after a train of men driving donkeys came along. They stopped in the usual way to talk. It is always easy to interest men in a practical matter like this, and the offer of a quarter dollar apiece made them eager to help. The stone was soon turned, revealing a dedication to the Boundary Gods of Apollonia, under Hadrian, A.D. 137. Then the messenger came up with half a dozen helpers ; and though there was no work for them, I paid them their hire, to their intense astonishment. To us that seems mere justice, to them it seemed mere folly. There was no limit to the madness of these Ingleez. Turks and Europeans can never judge alike. In their estimation the essential point was, why should two sets of men be paid for one piece of work ? That they had been brought a mile uphill was nothing to them—after they had done it—though much when you are trying to induce them to do it. If I had had my wits about me I should have explained the situation to them from the Oriental point of view : work had been promised them, and pay for it, but God had willed that the work should be done and the money earned by others, to whom he had granted it. Then, out of pure and undeserved liberality, I should have given them the money as a gift.   In this way they would have respected the action and the doer.   It is not so much what you do, as the way you do it, that helps you to be on friendly terms with the Turks.   They like far better to get money for nothing than to earn it ; to earn it is a degradation, and the paymaster a tyrant.   Put it in the light of a gift, and regard their service as a kindness, or a bit of hospitality to a stranger : they love the gift, and admire the generous giver.   On the other hand, your Scotsman hates to get money, unless he has earned it fairly ; the best of them won't take it, the worst of them take it and hate the giver.

At Apameia, the belief that the Ottoman Railway was coming soon had roused the spirit of activity and speculation.   A number of Greeks had already settled there.   Two khans had been built. Every one was eager to find out where the station would be placed, hoping to be first to buy land which would rise in value after the railway was made. As I was understood to know everything, many crafty schemes were put in operation to worm out of me the secrets of the railway plan ; but it was easy to conceal my knowledge, and gain credit for a deep one who could keep his own counsel, for, of course, I knew no more than they did. Others wanted to be recommended to my good friend, Mr. Walker, Chief Engineer of the O. R., and were so insistent and persistent as to become a serious nuisance. None ventured to ask a recommendation to the General Manager, Mr. Purser; he was understood to be a great and distant god, removed beyond the ken of mere men, and not to be lightly thought of.

Having been at Apameia about seventeen days previously with my wife, I had no prospect of finding anything fresh, and made an early start next morning. The distance to the railway terminus at Serai-Keui was called twenty-four hours, and I wanted to do it in two days. But with tired animals that was not an easy matter, and could only be achieved by steady plodding through two very long days. Hence, I did not devote several days to the proper exploration and study of the topography of Apameia as I ought to have done, since there was plenty of time before the next French steamer should start. I was still under the impression that the careful survey of a distinguished German professor, and the theory which he had founded on it, had exhausted the subject; and it was not until the vigorous sense of my friend the " Wandering Scholar" revolted at the central point in that theory, that I began to examine and test for myself. There was so much to do in Asia Minor that I at first grudged the time needed for districts that were readily accessible or had been already explored by others, thinking it better to accept their results, and to go on to the least known districts ; hence it has come about that the Lycos valley, through which I have gone fourteen times, is less known to me than most of the inner parts of Phrygia, and, so far as I may judge, the chapters of my *Cities and Bishoprics* that describe the Lycos valley are the least satisfactory and the least complete.   Many of my critics bring against me the opposite charge, that I have despised and rejected the work of my predecessors in recent times ; but the truth is that the lesson which cost me most time to learn was to test all theories, and not accept any until I had proved them on the spot; and my worst mistakes have been founded on theories accepted by the world in the dearth of evidence, and followed with blind faith by me. And the advice that I would impress on my successors in exploration is to accept nothing that I have said until they have tried it for themselves, to verify every inscription with critical eye on the outlook for faults, to test every statement and every description on the spot, but in doing so to be careful that they themselves are accurate. Only by long experience and many errors do you realise how hard it is to be accurate.   In strange surroundings, and with eyes unused to observe this class of facts (as all young travellers are), often in fatigue, almost in exhaustion, and in the nervous excitement produced by over-fatigue, in hurry and anxiety not to spend time unnecessarily, with the glowing sun gilding everything with its glamour and exercising on yourself its subtle but enervating charm, with food sufficient indeed for health but not sufficient to maintain that high standard of nervous energy that is required for your best work, you can hardly (and only unwillingly) recognise how error creeps in. You will look at a thing and see it wrong ; you may have the correct description before you, compare it with the original, and if you don't go over it a dozen times and look at it from all sides and in varieties of light, you may see wrong and pervert the facts. All these errors I have made myself, and seen others make. I have sometimes annoyed my coadjutors by insisting on verifying for myself their results, and been met by the accusation that I seemed to think their work of no account ; but I know that if they travelled for half a dozen years, they would .realise that I should have done better to be even more critical than I was. My own good fortune has lain in the fact that so many journeys and repetition of visits have enabled me to correct my own errors, and approximate to the truth as the mean of many varying observations.

Apameia is one of the most interesting places in the ancient world, and is likely to become a resort

of tourists.   It can be visited with ease and with perfect comfort, thanks to the Ottoman Railway.   But I
dare not begin here to describe it, or to tell how
you can see and hear its Laughing and its Weeping
Fountain, and visit the many other remarkable Fountains of the Marsyas, the Mæander, the Orgas,
and the Therma ; you can see where the goddess
Athena sat on the hill behind the city, and looking
down descried in the lake the mirrored distortion of
her face as she played on her newly invented flute ;
you may perhaps identify the rock from behind
which Marsyas peeped and saw her throw away the
flute in disgust ; you can certainly see the place
where he, on the accursed flute, tried to vie with
Apollo and his lyre, simple Phrygian matched
against civilised Greek; and you can sit under a
lineal descendant of the tree on which he was hung
up to be flayed by the hard-hearted victor in that
musical *agon*, and muse over the repetition of that
contest now going on around you, in which the
simple Mohammedan Phrygian is being vanquished
by the energetic, hard-working Greek settlers, and
accepts his defeat as " the will of Allah ".   But I
have elsewhere done what I can to set in its true
light and varied interest the long tale of Apameia-
Kelainai ;[1] and now we must hurry away to the
Ægean coast and the voyage home.

[1] *Cities and Bishoprics of Phrygia*, chs. xi., xii.

XV. To-day we rode down the "Great Eastern Highway" connecting the Ægean harbours with the eastern lands. During the first five hours there stretched on our left a country, partly hilly and partly plain, which has all the appearance of being able to support a large population, containing fully a dozen villages at the present day ; and yet I do not know that any traveller has ever gone through it. It lies near, yet off the line of, the Great Highway; and one would expect that it was formerly inhabited by a rather primitive people, like those of Tchal district. Then we went along the northern edge of the long salt lake Anava, where people still gather salt, as they did when the vast army of Xerxes marched by the same way. At ten hours we passed under the village Tchardak ; three weeks before my wife and I spent here the first night from Apameia ; but this time I plodded on two hours more to Bash-Tcheshme (Head-Fountain).

Bash-Tcheshme stands at the top of the pass that slopes down to the head of the Lycos valley. No stream runs down the pass (except while rain is falling), which in Byzantine times seems to have been called Graos Gala, Old-Woman's Milk, by coarse rustic wit. There is no village beside the fountain ; but merely a large shed, at which muleteers and drovers rest and purchase cups of coffee from the Turk who attends to the shed.

The only other products are dirt and fleas; but these are luxuriant.   The ground is alive with fleas; I have seen places that were pretty bad, but nothing to surpass Bash-Tcheshme.

This was, therefore, an excellent plan to test my recent discovery that waterproof keeps off vermin. I drew up my socks over my trousers, spread a waterproof sheet over the filthy mattress which the Turk gave me, put on my greatcoat, and over that a waterproof cloak; and lay down to rest quietly, undisturbed and victorious, till morning; while the armies of the enemy gathered round the sea of waterproof, and dared not cross.   The whole place was so indescribably filthy that I could not unfasten my own blankets.

XVI. Twelve hours to Serai-Keui, through the high glen of Colossai at the end of the upper glen of the Lycos, then down a long step to the lower Lycos valley.   At the eighth hour we passed the place where, three weeks ago, my wife and I were belated on the second night from Apameia and lay out for the night in a field; in the early morning, a shower coming on, we had to rise and take the road; and we rode into Serai-Keui, four hours distant, as the people were going to the station to take the early train starting at 7 A.M. Among them were some friends who had come up for a day from Smyrna with whom we acquired great but not wholly deserved credit for activity. This time my horse was pretty well exhausted, and his rider was not very fresh; but with the prospect of a good meal and a comfortable bed at Serai-Keui, we struggled on. There I paid off my men, and took the early train next morning for Smyrna, having done a hard sixteen days' work, and sustained some great disappointments, but consoled for all by the Jewish inscription.

CHAPTER V.

THE MOHAMMEDAN RACES OF ASIA MINOR.

ONE of the facts that are most striking to the traveller in Asia Minor is the interlacing and alternation of separate and unblending races. In half a dozen villages which you visit in the course of a day you may find four or five separate peoples, differing in manners, dress, language, and even religion, each living in its own village, and never intermarrying with, rarely even entering, the alien village a mile or two distant. The broad distinction of Christian and Moslem is wholly insufficient and even misleading. The Turkish peasants entertain a stronger hatred towards the Circassian, rigid and pious Moslem as he is, than towards the Greek or Armenian Christian, while they regard the Kizil-Bash or heterodox Turkmens with a mingled loathing and contempt, surpassing their worst scorn for the Christian. You often meet a Greek in a Turkish village, sitting in the Oda, apparently in quite friendly conversation with the people ; but you will hardly ever see a Turk in a Circassian village, and rarely a Circassian in a Turkish village, or, if you do, he glares about, feeling himself an enemy among enemies.

The same feature was noted by ancient observers in Asia Minor. Strabo speaks of the great variety of distinct races in Cappadocia about the Christian era, which implies that the same cause acted then as now, *viz.*, the races did not mix by intercourse and intermarriage. The tendency of Roman rule was to obliterate racial differences, and encourage homogeneousness ; and the same result was even more strongly fostered by the influence of the Church. Hence, in the fourth century, the great Cappadocian fathers, Basil and the Gregories, speak of the Cappadocians as if they were a single homogeneous race, different from and superior to the Galatians.

But since the Seljuk Turks entered Asia Minor in 1070, the conciliation of racial differences has ceased (except that those Christians, who accepted Mohammedanism, amalgamated with the immigrant Turks, as we shall see). All the different races that have swept over the unhappy land have left representatives in the existing population ; and all the different strains of blood remain unmixed.

I. TURKS.—Even those who call themselves Osmanli, or Ottoman Turks, and consider themselves homogeneous in race, present considerable varieties.

The Osmanli of the cities are very different in character from those of the villages, and those of one district vary widely from those of another. The Osmanli are almost the only example of real racial mixture under the Turkish *régime*. There can be no doubt that a considerable part of the Christian population of central Anatolia turned Moslem during the first two or three centuries of Turkish rule, and the Mohammedanised Christian population has melted into, or perhaps has absorbed into itself, the settled and more adaptable part of the Turkish population. In Phrygia and Pisidia, the Christian population disappeared almost entirely ; and the whole country became Mohammedan except a few small Christian settlements, *e.g.*, Zille beside Konia, Permenda beside Ak Sheher, Khonas near Denizli, quarters in the cities Sparta and Olu-Borlu, with one or two others. We see that the purely Christian city Laodiceia (pronounced Ladíkya), in A.D. 1210, had become the mainly Mohammedan city Ladik in 1332, and in 1340 had even lost its old name and taken the purely Turkish name Thingozlou (Deñizli, "full of waters ") ; and yet some of the old Anatolian institutions, such as "the Brotherhood," (see chapter xi.) remained in a Mohammedanised form. Further we find no reason to think that any violent change had occurred in the interval, for the .

Seljuk Sultans carried out no policy of extermination, but treated the Christian subjects so well that many of them fought valiantly against the oppressive Byzantine emperors. In view of facts like these, we must conclude that the population of cities like Ladik and Kutáya (Kotiaion) became Mohammedan in the mass, and that any Christian remnant dwindled or emigrated.[1]

The change was due, probably, to two reasons. In the first place, though no direct persecution of Christians was practised by the Turks, yet the position of inferiority aud degradation, to which the Christians were reduced, was such that a strong temptation existed to seek the easy, ever open entrance to honour and privilege. This alone, however, would have been insufficient without the second cause, which was that Phrygia had always been a hot-bed of heresy, and that all heretics were exposed to very harsh treatment at the hands of the Byzantine government. Many of these heresies were coloured by Oriental ideas; and a strong Oriental substratum existed in the population. Hence they were prone to relapse into a religion of the thoroughly Oriental type like Mohammedanism. On the other hand Cappadocia, where the Orthodox Church had been far more completely victorious, has a very much larger Christian population.

[1] *Cities and Bishoprics of Phrygia*, i., p. 25 ff.

That the change of religion took place in Phrygia and Pisidia, not at the movement of the Turkish conquest, but by gradual steps in the following period, is shown by the fact that we can often trace the existence of a Christian and a Mohammedan town side by side in a district which is now purely Mohammedan. So, for example, at five miles' distance from each other we find the Seljuk town Karamanli, "the men of Karaman" (a noted chief), and the Christian Tefeni, the town of Saint Stephen, and at one mile from each other Seljükler (the Seljuks) and Sivasli (the men of the Christian Sebaste). At the present day all are alike Moslem and Osmanli, and have been so for centuries ; but the names arose when the old Christians and the new Turks lived side by side, yet distinct, in the same valley.

From this point of view, every valley in Phrygia is a study in ethnology and in religious history, where names are the chief evidence of the changes which the historian tries to trace. Little has yet been done in this direction, for the view which has just been stated did not ripen in my mind till my travelling had ended, for a time at least ; and the generalisations, which are embodied and discussed in my book on the *Cities and Bishoprics of Phrygia*, grew in my mind during subsequent study. You can often trace, within one district, a Christian town moslemised, a Turkish town, and Turkmen, Circassian and recent refugee villages ; and all are recognisable by the names without entering them, while the first two can be distinguished only by the names.[1]

The Turkish part of the population, then, is very various in origin, Phrygian, Galatian, etc., mixed with true Turkish blood ; but this whole class regards itself as homogeneous, and its members mix freely.

After the Osmanli chiefs ousted the Seljuk Sultans, and reigned in their stead over a far vaster empire, the whole Turkish population began to style itself Osmanli ; and at the present day the name " Turk " is rarely used, and I have heard it employed only in two ways, either as a distinguishing term of race (for example, you ask whether a village is " Turk " or " Turkmen "), and as a term of contempt (for example, you mutter " Turk Kafa," where in English you would say " Blockhead ").

The contempt felt and expressed by Mohammedans of other races in the country for the Turks is a remarkable feature of which I have seen numerous examples. That excellent authority, " A Consul's Daughter and Wife,"[2] mentions a similar fact in Macedonia : " The Mohammedan Albanians deeply

---

[1] Many other examples are quoted *loc. cit.*, pp. 27, 303, 576, 581.
[2] *The People of Turkey*, i., p. 87.

resent the forfeiture of their liberty and the loss of their privileges. . . . The Albanian regards the Turk as a doubtful friend, and a corrupt and impotent master." Similarly, Circassians have said to me: " We fear the Russians much: we fear the English more: but we despise the Turks".

II. TURKMEN.—The Turkmen tribes are widely scattered through Anatolia. Already in the beginning of the thirteenth century, the historian Anna Comnena distinguishes correctly between Turks and Turkmens. The Turkmens are all nomadic, while the Turks lead a settled life. Yet it is certain that Turkmen villages occasionally put off the nomadic habit and adopt a settled life; but in that case, they tend to forget the name Turkmen, and to rank themselves as Turk and Osmanli. In the large valley of Metropolis (Tchul-Ova or Turk-men-Ova), I was told in 1883 that there was one Turk village, and all the rest were Turkmen. Now, most of them claim to be Turk: in one village, where we were very hospitably entertained in 1891, the magnate, who was by birth merely the Turk-men chief, admitted with some reluctance and shamefacedness, that the village had originally been Turkmen: doubtless his successor will believe that he is pure Osmanli.

This process, as I believe, has been going on for centuries, but it has been greatly quickened in recent years both by the policy of the government (which tries to discourage and even forcibly to stop nomadism), and by the marked growth of the European spirit in this Oriental land.[1] The question is, has it not been always going on? Is the original Turk (as distinguished from the Mohammedanised Phrygian or Galatian) anything more than a Turkmen after two or three generations of settled life? I put this question to Sir Henry Howorth and other authorities on a subject in which I am only an inquirer.

An intermediate stage between the nomadic habit of Turkmens and the settled habit of Turks is found in many villages and even towns, whose inhabitants, having in most respects the appearance of settled living, go partially out into summer quarters (Yaila). This custom of going to Yaila varies from the mild form, in which it is hardly more than a hygienic precaution (like the month or two in the country which is an institution among our own urban population), to the thorough-going style in which it is barely distinguishable from the nomadic habit; and the semi-nomadic habit exists in practically the same form among some Turkmens and some Turks who have long rejected the name Turkmen. Such facts point to an old-standing process whereby Turkmen becomes Turk in fact and in feeling.

1 See chapter vi.

These nomad Turkmen tribes are worthy the historian's attention. It was they, and not the Turkish armies, not even the terrible raids by which the Turks harried Byzantine territory, that destroyed the Roman civilisation and prosperity and population in Asia Minor. The Arabs raided all Asia Minor in as terrible a way for centuries, and were for long lords undisturbed of some parts of the country ; yet their conquest was ephemeral, and left no visible trace behind it. They won many battles, they destroyed cities, they lopped off territories from the Empire of the Caesars, but the fabric of Christian society was not affected by them. That great organisation, the result of Roman law and Christian teaching and ecclesiastical unity, defied all such assaults, and, like the hydra in the fable, it put forth a new head where one was lopped off; its flesh closed up and healed as soon as the sword had passed through it.

In like manner the fabric of Roman Christian society would, in all probability, have defied and outlasted the open attack of the Turks. After the first fury of their inroad was spent in the end of the eleventh century, it is obvious that the Byzantine armies were stronger than the Turkish, wherever they got a fair chance in the commanders who were put over them. Yet in spite of many defeats in detail, the Turkish power grew steadily stronger. The nomad Turkmens spread over the face of the land ; the soil passed out of cultivation; the population decreased ; the Christian cities were isolated from each other by a sea of nomad wandering tribes ; intercourse, and consequently trades and manufactures, were to a great extent destroyed ; and gradually the Christians in most places acquiesced, as we have seen, in the Oriental spirit and the Oriental religion of the dominant race. It is a remarkable instance of degeneration from civilised to barbarian society, and one which it would be instructive to study in detail ; but the general fact is summed up in the phrase, the nomadisation of Asia Minor.[1]

Turkmens are almost always exceedingly hospitable. In 1883, at lunch in a Turkmen tent a dozen miles south of Dorylaion, there was one man who struck me as being very Irish in appearance, and who was unusually pressing in his hospitality, inviting us most urgently to stay a night. I said to the friend who was with me that I had never met such cordial kindliness in all my experience, and remarked on the man's Irish look. As it was only midday, and there was no opening for work in the neighbourhood, we had to decline the invitation.

[1] *Cities and Bishoprics of Phrygia*, i., pp. 16 f., 27 ff., 299 ff., etc.

At night, while we were sitting at dinner, my friend said : " Would you be surprised to learn that that Turkmen whom you thought so like an Irishman speaks English as well as you or I do?" It turned out that, when we left, the man came out with us. I was in front, and he walked alongside of my friend's horse. After coming some little distance out of the camp, when there was no one near, he said, " You couldn't oblige me with a bit of to-bacco, could you, sir?" My friend gave him all that he had ; but did not ask him who he was, or how he came to be there. I was exceedingly vexed that we had not stopped at the encamp-ment : we might have had an interesting conversa-tion with that Irish Turkmen. It was obvious that he had come so far out of the camp in order to talk, and had selected my friend as having a speci-ally pleasant manner with natives : but the latter was so taken aback as to let the opportunity slip. I have often wished to go back to that camp.

A Turkmen Bey, who entertained us royally in 1882, gave us also an interesting account of his pilgrimage to Mecca.[1] He went twelve days' jour-ney through the Cilician Gates to Messina, where he found an English ship to take him to Port Said, thence through the Canal and down the Red Sea to Jeddah, the port for Mecca. There the *Dellil*

[1] I depended then on an interpreter.

of his district met him, took charge of him, brought him to a khan in Mecca and looked after him during his stay. His journey occupied rather more than four months and cost altogether £T.63 (about £57 stg.). In answer to a question, he explained that the *Dellils* were men who came from Mecca every second year collecting gifts for the holy shrine. Each of these had his special district, and wrote down the names of those in his district who intended to go on pilgrimage during the next two years, and each pilgrim when he came to Mecca inquired for his *Dellil*. He also said that the pilgrims paid nothing to the *Dellil* while they were in Mecca, but they were expected to send gifts afterwards, of which the *Dellil* received a portion.

Many of the Turkmen are Kizil-Bash (Red-Heads), *i.e.*, unorthodox Moslems : not merely is that the case with the nomads, but in many cases settled villages, where no trace of the nomadic habit remains, are Kizil-Bash, and loathed by the orthodox Turks.

III. YURUK.—The Yuruks are nomads, who are found in many parts of Asia Minor, but almost always, so far as my experience goes, in mountainous districts, whereas the Turkmen tribes usually live more in the great plains. According to Von Luschan, the Yuruks of Lycia are an immigrant race, akin to the Gypsies : his earlier view had been that they were Mongolian, but, in his final work on Lycia, he abandons his original opinion. I cannot pretend to hold any ethnological view ; but, while his later opinion seems in some respects startling and at first sight improbable, it has the merit of explaining the difference of haunts between Yuruk and Turkmen. Moreover, it is certain that there is a decidedly greater difference in character between Yuruk and Turkmen than there is between Turkmen and Turk.[1]

Differing from Dr. Humann, who declared that the Yuruks have no religion at all, Von Luschan maintains that they are good Mussulmans, regular in the five daily prayers, and in many cases going on pilgrimage to Mecca. My own experience is intermediate ; they do indeed claim to be Mohammedans, and practise circumcision, but I never saw a Yuruk praying in his own home, though, when they come into the settled villages, they put on all the appearance of good Moslems.[2] It is, however, possible, as Von Luschan remarks, that the Lycian Yuruks may differ in character from those of other regions known better to Humann and to me.

Von Luschan heard among the Yuruks a language different from Turkish. He is, doubtless, right; but I know nothing to confirm it. In general appear-

---

[1] *Reisen in Lykien*, etc., 1889, ii., p. 216 ff.
[2] So Sir C. Wilson, *Handbook, Turkey* (Murray), p. 68.

ance and way of talking they seemed to me very like the Turkmens. In 1880 I spent some days in a Yuruk winter village in Mt. Sipylos near Smyrna. After a very wet day, which much impeded exploration, I next morning asked the chief, a splendid-looking old man of about eighty, what he thought of the prospect of weather, thinking that his long experience would have made him weather-wise. His answer was in the true Turkish style, grave, measured, sententious: "How should I know the weather? God knows. If the sun shines, it will be fine weather; if it rains, the weather will be bad." So his answer was translated to me.

Dr. Von Luschan denies that intermarriage ever takes place between Yuruks and Turks. I have, however, known an example. In 1886 one of our men, named Veli, was a puzzle to me in character; he was always good-humoured and light-hearted, always good company, always idle, never to be trusted to do anything or take any trouble out of my sight, in short, utterly unlike a Turk. At last he could stand the work no longer, shammed illness, got himself laid up and doctored, and we went on without him. Our other man, Akhmet, one of the best Turks I have known,[1] explained matters. Veli was no Turk, but a Yuruk, who had married a woman of his village and settled down there. Akh-

[1] See p. 45.

met had great contempt for Yuruks, and thought them a useless and worthless lot; but he would not bring disgrace on Veli, so long as it might do him harm, and therefore told nothing until Veli had deserted.

That excellent traveller, Mr. Bent, gives an interesting account of the Yuruks of Taurus in the *Proceedings of the Royal Geographical Society*, 10th Aug., 1890, to which the curious reader may be referred. He attributes to them a more polygamous habit than I should have thought right, and he decidedly differs from Von Luschan as regards marriage, saying that they are not very particular where they steal a wife. He is, however, a better authority than I am on this point.

IV. AVSHAHR.—The Avshahrs are a race of strange history. Their chief seat is in the northwest of Persia; and Sir A. H. Layard gives a very interesting account of his experiences among them. Another considerable body of them now inhabits the Anti-Taurus range between the rivers Zamanti and Sarus. These formerly dwelt on the high rolling uplands between Sivas and Kaisari to the east of the river Halys, called the Uzun-Yaila (Long Summer-Quarters), where they maintained themselves in almost complete independence of the Turkish authority. The government profited by the Circassian immigration about thirty-five years ago to find a means of reducing the powerful and turbulent Avshahr. They presented the Uzun-Yaila to the Circassians, and bade them enter in and take possession. This was a thoroughly Turkish plan; whichever side conquered, the government would be rid of two troubles, for in a war between two such races the losers would be sadly broken in numbers and power, and even the winners would suffer severely. In the end, after a hard struggle, the remnant of the Avshahrs was driven into the Anti-Taurus, and the Circassians now own all the Uzun-Yaila.

Cooped up in these glens, the Avshahrs have lost much of the nomadic character; they are adopting the settled habit; and, shorn of their former power, they are far from being so free as they were on the Great Yailas. But even yet they are far bolder and prouder than the Turkish villagers. In 1882, when a zaptieh who was with us began to demand camp-requisites in his usual hectoring style, he was told to remember that he was now in the mountains, and that, if he uttered another word in that tone, they would beat him till he could not stand.

But there are other Avshahr villages in Asia Minor in which the recollection of racial character has been almost or entirely lost. It is not uncommon to find a village named Avshahr: in the valley of the Kazanes (Kara-Eyuk-Ova) there are two, distinguished as Avshahr and Kum-Avshahr.[1] In all such cases it is clear that a nomad group of Avshahrs has been stranded, and has settled down to village life ; the group was at first distinguished from surrounding peoples by its tribal name, and this has now become a mere appellation for the village.

V. RECENT REFUGEES.—The Circassians are in many respects the most interesting race in Asiatic Turkey. After the Russian conquest of the Caucasus, large numbers of the Mohammedan Circassians took refuge in Turkey, where the government promised them welcome and lands. Most of the immigrants learned to repent bitterly of having trusted a Turkish government promise. The officials, who were entrusted with the duty of settling them, went about their task in the usual style, promising always, performing nothing, aiming only at plundering the refugees of whatever they possessed. But the Circassians were not so submissive as Turks. Most of them took to robbery, and seized what they could find. One band, as I was told, who had been several times cheated by the Pasha at Amasia with promises of land, seized him in the government house, and compelled him by threats of death to execute a deed settling them on land in the district. Most

[1] Kum, Sand.

characteristic of Turkish policy was the way in which the main body was planted in the Long Yailas (see p. 109).

Similar, but much worse, has been the experience of the refugees from European districts, Bosnia, Bulgaria, etc., who came into Asia after the last war, 1878. This considerable accession should have added greatly to the strength of the country. The land is not half enough populated, and the population is dwindling. Yet the government could find nowhere to plant the refugees. They wandered over the face of the earth, and found no rest for the sole of their foot. In 1881 and later, we met many companies of them; and often they came weeping and entreating the help of the " English Pasha," who had been sent to introduce reforms into the country. Their tale was always the same: they had been sent to one place after another by the Turkish Refugee Commission : everywhere they had been refused by the people, and sent away : nobody would do anything for them : nobody would entertain them : their cattle were sold : their money was gone : they were starving. And this in a country naturally rich, fertile, and only half populated ! It seems strange to us of the north that these refugees should have been so slow to think of "the good old rule, the simple plan, that they should take who have the power ". But our people can never fully understand the obedient and peaceable spirit of the ordinary Orientals in such circumstances : men who have plenty of courage and make excellent soldiers will sit submissive to injustice and misery, regarding it as the will of God, where a northern race would at once rebel. Moreover, they were made powerless through separation, for the Refugee Commission, warned by former, experience with the Circassians, took care to break up the refugees into small parties.

At last, however, they were all settled : and the traveller will occasionally come across a village more than usually poor, yet differing in style from the abject misery and depression of the *tchiftlik* villages (p. 65) ; and the reason of this poverty is explained because the people, being refugees, have not yet been able to attain even the scanty and humble comforts of a Turkish village. The usual name of such villages is Mohajir-Keui (Refugee Village) ; the older inhabitants distinguish them in this way, and a historical fact is thus crystallised in the name. Similarly, one finds over the country numerous villages, Tcherkess-Keui, Abadza-Keui (Abadza are one of the Circassian tribes), etc. ; and thus a study of Turkish village names reveals a series of strata of population.

The Circassians, who have in many cases taken by force their present homes, have ever since been almost in a state of war with their Turkish neigh-bours, who regard them with intense hatred and fear. Your archæologist can hardly induce his Turkish servants to enter a Circassian village. In 1888 my wife and I, reaching a Circassian village at noon after a six hours' ride, stopped to lunch. We sat down in the verandah of a house; our two servants put up our horses and disappeared. We spent near three hours talking with a number of Circassians, who gathered round. All Circassians have a great natural faculty for geography, and good intellectual power generally; and they are therefore always interesting to talk to. One young fellow, a stranger stopping, like us, in the village, had travelled widely, and we had a long and animated discussion whether he or I had seen more of Turkey. When we intimated a desire to go on, the Circassians got ready our horses, brought them, and were ex-traordinarily cordial. We rode out of the village, and about a quarter of a mile on found our two ser-vants waiting with their own horses, starving and unhappy. That, however, was the worst case of terror that I have known.

Many have had a less pleasant experience among the Circassians than we. They are very expert horse thieves; and one hears many tales of their exploits in that way. A friend of ours had a horse stolen from the door of a wayside coffee-house, into which his servant had gone for a short time, leaving the horse fastened outside.

The most ingenious and clever case I heard about happened to a Turk, who was bringing a fine horse down to Smyrna to sell. He was told far up the country that some Circassians were following him to steal the horse; but declared that he took so good care that he did not fear them. Every night he fettered his horse with chains, and slept close beside it. So the days passed. On the night before reaching Smyrna the weather was chilly, and the Turk put his thick coat over the horse's back. In the morning, he rose and proceeded to take off the irons in order to lead the horse to water. As he unfastened them, the horse started off at a headlong pace, the coat dropped off and disclosed a Circassian underneath it, who rapidly disappeared from sight.

VI. Kurds.—My earlier experiences of the Kurds were unfavourable. In the Haimane district, the high-lying plains and hills, south of Angora, several tribes of Kurds live a nomadic and more or less independent life. They made on me the impression of being ruder in manners, more niggardly and grasping, and less hospitable, than Turks or Turkmens. I remember in August, 1883, with Prof. Sterrett, visiting the great Bey of the western Haimane Kurds; and he entertained us with what

he called sherbet, which was only dirty-looking
water sweetened with sugar.   Sterrett manfully
drank his glass, and kept up our credit for decent
manners ; but I could not get the stuff down.
The same general type of character seemed to rule
everywhere we met them ; and in 1886 Brown and
I, crossing the Eastern Haimane, spent a night at
the camp of the other great Bey, and I acquired a
positive dislike for Kurds.   They were not inhospitable : they sold us all we wanted, and invited us
to call on the great man, close to whose tent ours
was pitched.   But they were to me repellent ; and
I doubt if I could ever have been able to get on
friendly terms with them.

The Kurds of the Haimane had the reputation
of being very unruly and dangerous.   At one time
they were practically independent, and paid no
tribute ; but now they are more peaceable.   It
seemed advisable in 1883 to take a zaptieh, in order
to have some show of authority, while we were
wandering in this district.   He told us that the
Kurds were now perfectly quiet, and travelling was
quite safe : it had been very different formerly, but
the present *Kaimmakam*, a Circassian, had .taught
them a lesson : he could not, of course, get
authority to execute any of them (p. 149), but he
had a practice of beating severely any one that
was arrested, and it chanced that every one after

being beaten died, and the Haimane was now at rest.

This was one out of many instances, in various parts of the country, of the immense effect produced by one or two examples of rigour. As soon as it comes to be known in any district that the reins of power are in a firm hand, and that disorder will be punished, the whole country under that governor becomes as peaceable and quiet as any part of Britain ; but such governors are very rare, for a governor has usually other fish to fry. The Circassians are the most difficult to keep in order; and they furnish a larger proportion of the thieves than any other class ; their principle is the motto of the old Border family, " Thou shalt want ere I want ".

The Kurds of the Euphrates country impressed me much more favourably than those of the Haimane ; but I have seen far less of them. In 1890, Hogarth and I, crossing their country, had the reputation of being engineers prospecting for a railway ; and the idea of a railway is almost always highly popular. Every one knows that a railway brings money, and openings for work and earning, and increases the value of land. Many people also, not Christians alone, welcome a railway as the herald of a new form of government *à la Franga*, in which Europeans shall renovate the country. Every

Kurd village welcomed us effusively, and at one village the son of the Bey said to one of our servants: "All our men are thieves, but if you lose anything, come to me, and I will get it back for you". Hospitality and frankness could go no further than that.[1]

Professor Sterrett, however, who crossed the same country in 1884, says: " The whole mountain country between Arga and the Tokluna Su is inhabited solely by Kurds, an inhospitable, murderous set of filthy villains, who still preserve all the ferocious characteristics of their ancestors, the ancient Kardouchoi, of whom Xenophon has little good to report in the *Anabasis* "; and he wrote to me at the time that his whole party had a narrow escape from them.

VII.—The number of minor varieties of people who are, or to the superficial traveller might seem to be, Mohammedan is large, Noghai (pronounced Noi) and other Tatars, Ansarieh (of whom Disraeli gave such a glowing and high-coloured description in *Tancred*), Yezidi or Devil Worshippers, etc. But, as I have come little, or not at all, into relations with them, except the Tatars (a quaint, always amusing people of low intellectual calibre, but not unpleasant to deal with, so long as you don't expect much from them), they do not enter into the plan

---

[1] A supposed Kurd, p. 48.

of this book. The Takhtaji, a strange people, are briefly described in chapter xi.

The most marked way in which difference of race makes itself obvious to the traveller is in the appearance and action of the women. In one village you will observe that the women are closely veiled and keep themselves absolutely apart. If they see you at a distance they get out of the way ; if you come suddenly upon them, they veil themselves more closely, turn their faces towards the wall, and stand so till you have passed ; but curiosity is strong, and if you turn and rudely cast a glance over your shoulder after passing, you will generally see that they are gazing at the strange horsemen, and you make them again hastily veil themselves. Some of them, however, seem so hopelessly broken in spirit by the continuous drudgery which constitutes the life of a peasant Turkish woman, that they have lost the power to take any interest in anything.

In the next village, a mile or two away, the women may leave their faces uncovered, mingle freely with the men, and readily converse with strangers. Among all the nomadic or semi-nomadic races, freedom and openness characterise the women more or less ; these preserve the real old Turkish custom. The Turkish tribes originally did not practise the seclusion of women; they learned that custom from the Arabs and the Koran, and perhaps also from the Greeks, among whom women were confined to a very retired life. It is only among the Osmanli Turks of cities and settled villages that seclusion is rigorously practised.

It was once my lot to spend some time in the sole company of a number of Avshahr women. Crossing the Anti-Taurus mountains in 1882 with Sir Charles Wilson, we came to a group of milestones by the roadside, a few miles east of Comana. As the rest of the party were in a hurry, and it seemed to me necessary to stay some considerable time and make impressions, I was left behind with a zaptieh. While the impressions were drying on the stones, a sudden very heavy thunderstorm came on; and we took refuge, much against my will, in an Avshahr village half a mile away. I felt uneasy lest some trouble might arise, for the zaptieh was the man who had got into difficulties at another Avshahr village two days before (p. 109). Armed with a waterproof, I did not mind the rain; but the zaptieh did; and I did not like to make him go on. We entered a house, in which there was no one but an elderly woman; and I sat down on the cushions which she spread, while the zaptieh bustled about, talked to her, and found out that there were "written stones" in an inner chamber. I went in, and found that, while the outer room was a wooden hut, built of rough logs, with chinks through which the wind whistled, the inner room was to a considerable extent dug out of the hill side, and contained a large fireplace, the two side stones of which were splendid Roman milestones. The zaptieh and the old woman remained in the outer room talking. Having hurriedly copied the stones, I returned and found that the zaptieh had gone, leaving me alone with the woman. I found the situation embarrassing. Among the Turks one learns to respect scrupulously their customs in regard to women and to religion; and it becomes almost second nature to think as they do. But in this case, on the analogy of Turkish houses, I thought that the outer room was the public room (*selamlik*), while the inner chamber was more private and sacred to the women and the family life; and it seemed proper to return as soon as possible to the *selamlik*, even though there was a solitary woman there. I had hardly sat down, when a dozen women came in, eager to see the stranger: some sat on the floor, others stood round, and I became aware that a score more, less bold or more youthful, were peeping through the doorway and the chinks of the wall. This was still more perplexing: if a few

Avshahr chiefs should return, and object to the situation, it would be difficult to explain my conduct satisfactorily. It was all the more embarrassing that I could find nothing to say to the women. I knew very little Turkish at that time (having as yet always had the aid of a Greek or English-speaking interpreter); all the words and phrases fled from me except " How old are you ? " But I could not venture on so personal a question, not knowing in what spirit it might be received ; and the reception which the zaptieh's impertinence to the Avshahr men had met with two days ago made me think with alarm about the consequences of addressing any dangerous question to the women. The seclusion of women began to assume unsuspected excellences in my estimation; and I longed to have it made universal in Asia Minor. One thing was clear : those who were in the room had no objection to being stared at, and no reluctance to stare at me. One woman brought a piece of carpet, spread it carefully close in front of me, sat down on it, and gazed long and steadily in my face. I was profoundly thankful when the rain slackened and the zaptieh returned, and we could begin our ride of eight hours across the mountains to rejoin the main body.

The incident, trifling in itself, is worth recounting in order to bring out how much depends on knowing the ways of the people among whom one is travelling : even after being two and a half years in Turkey, I was quite nonplussed by Avshahr customs. The impressions of a traveller to whom everything is strange are very apt to spring from his own mind more than from the real facts.

The most depressing and melancholy part of the traveller's Turkish experiences relates to the women and their position. As a rule, the peasant women have such a hard life of constant work from a very early age, their life is so devoid of relief, of enjoyment, of educating or humanising influences, they seem so tattered, ragged, forlorn, and uncared for, as they stand with their face towards a mud wall while you ride past, that indignation and disgust grow strong in your mind against the social system that treats women in this way. A Greek-speaking Albanian servant, Akhmet, whom we had with us in Oct., Nov., 1881, pointed to a herd of Turkish women toiling like beasts of burden near a village, and remarked with a world of scorn in his tone: "Thus are the Turks: the wife of Akhmet sits at home". It would be difficult to live much among the peasants without learning to sympathise with the "Women's Movement" in more civilised lands. The total want of pleasant intercourse and friendly open relations between men and women greatly intensifies the monotony and the ignorance of village life, and also produces many other evils—a subject on which I will not enter. But after a long time among Turks, it was quite delightful and refreshing to meet, beside a Kurd village, a young man driving out a bullock-cart to the harvest, and a young woman walking beside it, talking and laughing and engrossed in each other's company. It was like a breath of Europe, bearing the scent of home.

CHAPTER VI.

PAST AND PRESENT IN ASIATIC TURKEY.

THE aim of these unpretending sketches is simply to describe what I have seen in Turkey, as it now is; but in order to suggest the real meaning of the present facts and how much importance lies in accurate observation of the small things that pass before the traveller's eyes, it is necessary to point out the relation which the present bears to the past.

At the present day the central movement in Asia Minor is, what it always has been, a conflict between the Eastern and the Western spirit. The oldest fact that we can gather in its history is the crossing over from Europe of Phrygian and Thracian tribes, who, seizing on part of the country, either ruled it as a dominant caste or amalgamated in varying degrees of strength with the native population. The poet of the Iliad conceived the war of Troy as the war of Greek against Asiatic, *Graecia barbariae lento collisa duello;* and Herodotus in his opening chapters describes the steps in the long conflict between Europe and Asia, culminat-

(124)

ing in the gigantic effort made by Xerxes to strike down the Greeks, and the decisive victory of the disciplined few over the barbarian multitudes at Salamis, Plataea, and Mykale. After that supreme effort on the part of Asia, the power of Europe grew stronger in the Debatable Land of Asia Minor, until, guided by the genius and inspired by the lofty ideals of Alexander the Great, it swept over Asia far beyond the Debatable Land even up to the Himalaya mountains and the Indus valley. But a wave like that ebbed almost as fast as it had overflowed ; Central Asia was overrun, but was practically unaffected by Greek civilisation ; even in Asia Minor Oriental reaction was led by Mithridates. Rome came to the aid of Greece, caught the torch of Western civilisation from Greek hands, and was busy for centuries organising and governing and training in western ways the peoples of Asia Minor. But to facilitate their work, the Romans had to adapt their administration to the people ; and it was not an unmixed western character that was imparted to the land. It is true that the great cities put on a western appearance and took western names ; Latin and Greek were the languages of government, of education, and of polite society. But this appearance was still only superficial. Greek had not become the popular language (apart from the Christians) even in the third century after Christ: the mass of the pagan peoples in the country districts spoke Phrygian and Lycaonian and Cappadocian ; though those who wrote wrote in Greek, and the officials governed by the use of Greek and Latin.

The Christian religion did what Rome had failed to do : it imposed on the people its own language, in which its sacred books were written, Greek. The western spirit became far stronger in the fourth century than ever before ; and it is a strangely mixed and interesting picture of eastern Asia Minor that is revealed to us in the pages of the great Cappadocian fathers, Basil and the Gregories. But even the Church was not strong enough to separate the Debatable Land completely from Asia and to associate it thoroughly with Europe. The popular Christianity of Phrygia was never like the Christianity of Europe. Sects of enthusiasts who perpetuated or revived the Oriental character in their religious forms always flourished there ; the Orthodox writers inveigh against the many heresies of Anatolia ; and the Orthodox Church had to permit in the worship of local saints the native characteristics, which they had failed to eradicate.

In the Byzantine period, after the time of Justinian, there was a slow but steady revival of the Oriental spirit, signs of which are apparent to the scholar in every department of life. In the seventh century, or later, many of the Greek city names disappeared, and old native names were revived. In the political sphere, the great and strong machine of organised government, which Roman genius and skill had constructed, was not easily destroyed and lasted for many centuries. But, as time passed on, the character of the government slowly changed, and the Western element grew weaker; dynasty succeeded dynasty, and each was more Oriental in type than its predecessor. Under the titles of Roman Emperors, Phrygians, Isaurians, Cappadocians, Armenians were masked, until at last the final step was taken, and the Turk sat on the throne of the Roman Augusti, or rather of the Romaic Sebastoi.

That last change was not so great as it is sometimes represented. The genius of the country tends always towards the same goal; for centuries it had been moving towards it; and about A.D. 1070, most of Asia Minor became Oriental in language and in government. The region of Constantinople, separate now from the mass of Asia Minor, preserved for a long time the " Romaic " forms, and was in some respects less Oriental than before, for Greek dynasties, like the Palaiologoi, Greek in name and repute at least, and no longer unmistakably Phrygian or Armenian, ruled at Constantinople, and maintained for three centuries and a half the struggle whether Turk or Roman should govern the western fringe and the coast lands of Asia Minor. But in 1070 the battle of Manzikert had laid the main mass of Asia Minor prostrate and helpless at the feet of the Seljuk Turks; and their right to it was formally acknowledged by the weak claimants to the Romaic throne in the following years. From that time dates the practically unbroken rule of the Turks over most of the inner country, though the Romaic Empire lasted at Constantinople till 1453; and in the twelfth and following centuries Turkish names for old Graeco-Roman cities of the land are often employed even by Byzantine historians. Kolonia is now called Axara or Taxara, the Turkish Ak-Serai, "White Mansion" (with or without the Greek definite article before it); Iconium is spoken of as Tokonion, the Turkish Konia (with Greek definite article prefixed); occasionally, the Greek name having been lost, the Turkish name takes its place and is translated by Byzantine historians, as in Mavrokastro (Kara-Hissar) or Neokastro (Yeni-Kale): and we find the pure Turkish names Ak-Sheher, Bey-Sheher, etc., spelt in Greek letters, just as, at the present day, one may see over the door of a Greek Church in a Cappadocian Christian village an inscription in Greek lettering but in pure Turkish language. Then, too, many old Oriental names for great cities, names most of which had disappeared from educated speech and official usage for 1000 years, return into use ; and it becomes evident that our superficial idea, derived from literature, that these names had been lost and forgotten, is wholly erroneous : the common people had retained the Oriental names, and had never accepted the Greek or Roman titles : the Turks found the Oriental name still vigorous in the popular mouth, and at the present day the Greek name is forgotten, except perhaps in some official Church lists, while the ancient name is used by all. Such are Marash (Marasion in Cinnamus and Anna Comnena), Kharput (Kharpote in Cedrenus), etc.

For nearly eight centuries the Oriental element reigned supreme and unopposed in Asia Minor ; Orientalism, revenging the conquests of Alexander the Great, had swept far into Europe, and the contest between East and West was maintained, not on the Euphrates or the Halys, but on the Danube. But, step by step, Asia has been driven back, out of Greece, out of the Danube valley, across the Balkans ; and now the armies are being marshalled for the last war,[1] which shall set South-eastern Europe free from the incubus that has oppressed it ; and in Asia Minor the old struggle has recommenced.

[1] This was written in reference to the general situation of the last decade, not to the single phase of the Greek war.

About 1820-1830, when part of European Greece was set free, the Greek movement in Asia Minor was for the moment restrained by the usual Turkish policy, by massacres like that in Scio, when the island was given up to pillage and slaughter: the city of Scio and about fifty villages, not to mention many churches and monasteries, were burnt to ashes; the leading clergy and citizens were hanged in mockery of legal forms; 30,000 people were massacred within two months; 32,000 were made slaves; 30,000 destitute refugees escaped to other lands; and a miserable remnant of people were left[1] in that once rich, industrious, and splendid island, a centre of education and commerce.

By means like this, the Turks for a time prevented and postponed the development of Greek feeling; but it was only for a time. On the west coasts of Asia Minor, the Greek element has increased immensely in strength, while the Turkish element has grown weaker. Every one who has any familiarity with the Aeolic and Ionian coasts knows of many a flourishing Greek village, which not so many years ago was empty or peopled only by Turks. The Turks are losing, or have in places

---

[1] It is well known that a prominent and accomplished Turkish official in high civil rank at Constantinople is the son of a young Sciote boy, saved at the massacre by a Turkish officer, and adopted by him.

lost, their hold on the coast and on the valleys that open on the coast. The Oriental element does not retreat or emigrate ; it is not driven out by force ; it dies out in these parts by a slow but sure decay ; you can only say that here the people was, and here it has almost ceased to be. As the railway goes inland, the Greek element goes with it and even in front of it. Trade is from the first almost entirely in their hands. Even where the capital is foreign, the practical working is to a great extent directed by Greeks. Soon the land, too, passes into their hands. Your village Turk is helpless and improvident. It is a point of honour with him to make a great show at a marriage. He borrows money, usually to make a display at some ceremonial, to buy a substitute in the conscription, or to give in bribery to an official : then his ruin is speedy, and the land on whose security he has borrowed passes out of his possession.

When we first visited the Lycos valley in October, 1881, the railway had not gone up so far. In Serai-Keui we were entertained by a Greek, who told us that he was the only Christian in the village,[1] and that he had come there as agent for one of the two railways, which competed for the trade of the

[1] Arundel mentions that a few Greek houses existed in Serai-Keui in 1826.

valley. In 1882, or early in 1883, the railway line was opened as far as Serai-Keui, and Serai-Keui has steadily grown Greek. Turkish statistics for 1894 give its Greek population as 450; but this was probably too low an estimate. Growth in Turkey is, of course, always slow.

The Ottoman Railway has now gone up beyond Serai-Keui some seventy miles, to Ishekli (Eumeneia) and to Dineir (Apameia-Celaenae); and the same process is going on all along the line. In 1891 we were hospitably entertained at a commodious and comfortable country house, four hours from Dineir, standing on an estate which was the property of a European Levantine family: in 1883 the spot was a waste, uncultivated and forlorn, where we hunted for inscriptions in a deserted, solitary cemetery. Fifteen or sixteen hours east of Dineir, in a Pisidian valley, on the head waters of the Eurymedon, where, probably, no Christian set foot for centuries, we found in 1890 a *tchift-lik* (estate), belonging to a Greek family resident at Egerdir near Sparta: there was a considerable degree of activity perceptible about it, and a score or more of rude inscriptions in an unknown Pisidian dialect, found in the digging and building operations carried out by the new Greek owners, had been collected in an outhouse, which thus was constituted into a rough and rude museum. It is characteristic of the Greek spirit and the admiration of even the rudest and least educated Greeks for antiquities and education, that on this outpost of Greek life in the Turkish mountains there should be already what you might call a museum, even though it was only a rough shed, used for storing other things as well as antiquities.

The steady, inexorable, irresistible spread of European, and mainly of Greek, influence in the western parts of Asia Minor, is by far the most striking fact in modern Turkey. That progress is so patent that the Turks make practically no attempt to resist it: it is accepted as inevitable. The Asiatic Greeks have the future in their hands ; and no man or no policy will be successful, which does not recognise that fact and build upon it as foundation. It has often come home to me, and I have often pointed out to fellow-travellers, that as soon as a few Greek traders establish themselves in a district of Western Anatolia, the Turkish governor who tries to go against them has not a dog's life of it. They play into each other's hands; and they have on their side the Turk's despair in his own future and his belief that " Reform " (the word is terribly familiar to him ; it is the fetish which he would fain propitiate) must come, and that, as it comes, it will sweep him away. The subject Greek feels that the world is with him; the Turkish governor feels that it is against him.[1]

The first thing that impressed me, when I began to learn something of Turkish feeling in 1880-1881, was the hopeless despondency which was openly expressed about the future of the country. Prophecies were current that the term of Turkish power was at hand. Everywhere one observed signs of the same feeling that prompted the saying of a *bin-bashi* ("head over a thousand," an officer corresponding in rank to a major in the British army) at Angora—"We have deserved the ruin that is surely before us and nothing can save us". I have known soldiers who fought in the last Russo-Turkish War declare that the misfortunes which befell the Turks were a just punishment for the treatment of the wounded Russians by their own men (especially by the irregular troops). Although the best troops in the Turkish army—and excellent troops they are—come from Anatolia, I never heard those who had served express anything but dislike of warfare, and a devout wish that they might have no more of it. Not the slightest sign ever came

[1] This refers to the period when I knew Turkey personally, ending in 1891. I have some reason to believe that the Mohammedan revival, carefully engineered from the palace, has grown steadily since then.

under my notice of anything like *esprit de corps*, or of that pride in the service which rarely fails in an old soldier of our army. The nearest approach to it I ever saw was in an old man whom I doctored with quinine at a guardhouse on a trade road in Pontus (said to be rather infested by robbers). He had fought under General Williams at Kars against the Russians, and described with great feeling the kindness, the self-sacrifice, and the bravery of the English general, declaring that he would never believe anything bad of the English.

This feeling was, doubtless, due in part to the complete destruction of their armies by the Russians in the recent war ; and so far as that was the cause, the feeling might be only temporary. But I believe that it arose much more from the settled conviction that their system of government was bad. The idea of "Reform," even the word, had become familiar to them by frequent reiteration ; they believed in its necessity, but not in its possibility. Of course, the ordinary villagers had not risen to such a pitch of reasoning power as to consciously think like this ; they knew nothing except their village concerns, their fear of the officials, and their dislike to the thought of being forced away from home to fight. But in towns, where a little was known of the outside world, that was the general tone.

In 1882 a change was very marked, and has been so ever since. There began a distinct revival of Mohammedan feeling. The prophecies current were no longer about the term of *Turkish* power, they were that the year 1300 (beginning 31st Oct., 1882) was an epoch of *Mohammedan* power, bringing either new life and strength or utter and complete ruin. The change of adjective, no longer *Turkish* but *Mohammedan*, was significant of much that was to follow. The skilful variation in the old prophecy reminds one of the old Athenian oracle which was adapted by people at the opening of the Peloponnesian War to suit their own conception of the course of events, some reading *loimos* (pestilence), while others declared that *limos* (famine) was the right word. So in Turkey in 1882, it was no longer the *Turkish* rule that was spoken of, "it was the Mohammedan [1] power that was at its crisis, and the people who never would have willingly raised their hand in support of their race were eager in defence of their religion. There can be no doubt that such a complete revolution of feeling was the result of a skilfully planned agitation directed from some centre. Hatred of the English was especially strong; indeed I cannot affirm that I saw actual proof of much feeling

[1] I purposely quote the following words verbatim from a paper which I published in the *Scotsman*, 16th September, 1882.

against other Christians ;[1] and certainly this hatred
was more conspicuous among the Government
officials than among any other class of the people.
When the news once came that a Turkish pasha
had defeated an English fleet and destroyed many
ships, the rejoicing was great ;" and great uneasiness as to possible disturbances was felt in some
non-Turkish circles. It was instructive to note
the sudden fall in the emotions of the Turks, when
the news of the bombardment of Alexandria and
the complete defeat of the Mohammedan forces
could no longer be disbelieved. The German
consul in a Turkish city told us shortly afterwards
"that for months previously the English had been
the object of most virulent language there ; but
when the news arrived, there was a sudden lull.
There is, however, little doubt that any disaster
to our army in Egypt might have produced wide-
reaching consequences through Turkey."[2]

A friend, a foreign consul, who united with the
education of a European observer the intimacy of
a native with Turkish affairs, mentioned to me
that the *Dellils* (see p. 105), who in former years
were common people, illiterate and ignorant, mere

---

[1] Those who lived in the more eastern parts of Turkey did see
it and bear witness.

[2] Again quoted, with omission of some unimportant words
from the same article, *Scotsman*, 16th September, 1882.

itinerant gatherers of alms, began about 1882 to be persons of a different class. They were educated men, with whom begging was a mere pretence, and who stirred up the people to make a great effort for the regeneration of the Mohammedan power.

That was the beginning, so far as outsiders like me could observe, of a movement that has gone on continuously since. It has been prominent chiefly in the eastern parts of Anatolia, and the region towards Constantinople. It has not so much affected the Greek districts towards the west, though great uneasiness has existed there, and no reasonable being can doubt that the process, if successful in the east, will spread to the west. It is a temporary revival of Orientalism, similar to that which took place under Mithridates, and not unlike it in the method, *viz.*, the attempted extermination of all who are affected by the Western spirit. But, in this case, dread of European armies shields the life of European residents ; whereas Mithridates began by a general massacre of all Romans in Asia Minor.

Naturally, one cannot be a listener to the sermons that are preached ; but the impression made on myself and on better observers has been, that the directors and preachers of the faith in Turkey have been engaged for a good many years in preparing the Mohammedan revival; the means whereby Turkish power is restored is always the same—massacre—and the preparation consists in preaching that it is a virtue and a merit before heaven to slay and spoil the infidels.

Further, it is not, so far as I know, doubted by any one who is familiar with Turkey, that this revival of Orientalism had been planned and directed from one centre, and that the effects seen since 1882 are the result of long preparation. This great historical movement is due to the will and the wit of that remarkable man, the present Sultan, who alone did not despair of the state, but with marvellous patience and hard work and diplomatic skill, set himself to strive against fate. Shelley, in his *Hellas*, puts into Sultan Mahmud's mouth the words :—

> Even as that moon
> Renews itself—shall we be not renewed ;
> Far other bark than ours were needed now
> To stem the torrent of descending time.

But Sultan Abd-ul-Hamid believed that the Crescent would be renewed, and he has for twenty years faced the torrent in his shattered and hardly seaworthy bark, kept her head upstream, and made astonishing way. With an almost bankrupt treasury, a navy which has rotted till the ships hardly hold together, a beaten and broken army, a disaffected people, surrounded by disloyalty, in constant peril from his own subjects, held on his throne only by the diplomatists of Europe and their mutual hatred and mistrust and the dread of each that another may secure their coveted share of dismembered Turkey, he reigns still, the sole mover of Turkish policy, autocrat to a degree that no other recent Sultan has been; and under him Mohammedanism and Orientalism have gathered fresh strength to defy the feeling of Europe, strength lying in the moral power that resolute purpose and religious fervour give against selfish or blundering adversaries.

He gauged the situation from the first ; he saw that the party of Reform in Turkey was hastening on the dissolution of Ottoman rule, for a reformed Turkey was a contradiction in terms. He saw that Reform was inconsistent with a Sultan of the Ottoman type, that Sultan and Khalif were united in one person, and that, when there ceased to be a Khalif in Constantinople, then Mohammedanism in Europe and in Asia Minor was doomed. He saw too that English policy was always and necessarily directed to secure Reform, that the dream of English statesmen and their watchword were always " a reformed and strong Turkey," that the Young Turkish party of Reform was the Anglophile party, and that its strength lay in the general belief that it had England to support it; in short, that England was the arch-enemy of all that he believed in and desired. From the first day when his influence began to be felt, he has worked and watched, prayed and waited, intrigued and chosen his allies, with the view of destroying English influence in Turkey. Step by step he has first weakened and then destroyed his enemies; and in most of his steps he has had the help of some party in England, which was induced to ruin English influence under the mistaken idea that it was furthering "British interests".

It is no recent theory of my own that is here stated: it is what has been said to me many a time in the years 1880-1884, when I was residing almost continuously in Turkey, by men of great experience in the country, men of many nationalities. Some spoke with regret, some with indifference, some with satisfaction, but all with conviction: "your government seems never to recognise that the Sultan is its great and bitter enemy; and so it is always playing into his hands".[1]

That is the reason why the Sultan has found friends in Russia and in every enemy of Britain. He has been playing the game which they desire to see successful: he has been preventing Asia

[1] The same ideas were expressed in a series of papers which appeared in the *Scotsman*, 1882, and fifteen years only confirm what I then wrote.

Minor from passing under British influence. Lord Salisbury protests in the strongest terms that Britain has never entertained any schemes of acquisition in Asia Minor. In the first place, however, there is probably no Russian or German or Frenchman who believes him ; and they say that, after he came to the Berlin Congress pretending to be free from all engagements, while all the time he had up his sleeve a private bargain with the Turks about the very subject which was to have been settled by the Congress, his assertions as to clean hands can no longer be trusted. Secondly, there was probably no man in Asia Minor of any nationality about 1879 to 1882, who was not looking forward to and forecasting the probability of the country passing into British hands, and the existence of this belief in the country was undoubtedly known to the European Powers. Thirdly, events were for a time all tending in that way ; and any statesman who declares that he was not aware of or affected by the drift of popular feeling and the tendency of events in Asiatic Turkey, is protesting to the European powers that he was careless of the elementary facts of the situation. Rightly or wrongly (I cannot pretend to decide) there is everywhere abroad, as my correspondents in various countries have always assured me, the belief that Lord Salisbury was a much craftier statesman than he will allow, that he knew much which he now ignores; and the protestations that Britain entertains no designs in Asia Minor merely make people abroad all the more sure that a British statesman's word can never be trusted.

And when one looks at the facts, how can they think otherwise? When both Turkey and Russia were exhausted with the war of 1877-78, Britain stepped in, and like the lawyer seized most of the oyster for which they had been contending, and gave them each a shell. She was left in possession of Cyprus (which needed only the expenditure of a sum, large indeed, but an insignificant detail in an English Budget, to be made an important point with a new harbour), holding the Protectorate of Asia Minor, champion of the Christians in Armenia, checking by a system of military consuls the administration of the country. The Porte was powerless to resist, and could only obey. The aspirations and hopes of the Christians, in whom lay the real strength of the land (except in open battle)—hopes which had previously rested on Russia—were now turned towards England as having guaranteed good government for them, and having prevented Russia from undertaking the guarantee. Britain had planted herself upon all the lines of development in the country, and all its strongest forces were pushing her on. A new department was created ; a series of young consuls, selected by competitive examination annually, went out to Turkey in regular course to learn the languages of the country before beginning their official work. As a piece of statesmanship, crafty and unscrupulous, but able, it was a master-stroke'; though I think no one among us will ever look back to it without blushing for the jockeying by which it was effected. But it was that kind of stroke which neither of the parties who had been cheated could forget or forgive. If Lord Salisbury claims that he never had any designs in Asia Minor, he is claiming to have been a mere dummy, pushed forward by Lord Beaconsfield, and entirely ignorant of the meaning of what he was doing. The foreigners believe that he was an abler man than that ; perhaps they are wrong ; but there is some justification for their error, and its existence has been a notable factor in the situation since he came back to power. There was in 1895 a possibility that the Liberal foreign minister might have been trusted not to be concocting some stroke of acquisitiveness ; nobody had ever imagined him to be guilty of any great stroke, and this belief was a safeguard in that delicate situation. But there was no possibility that Russia should trust a man, whose very protestations were understood by her as proofs of duplicity.

The only way in which Britain could atone for the cunning that had given her so strong a position in Asia Minor was by using that position for the advancement of civilisation and the benefit of the peoples of Asia Minor, just as she has used her position in Egypt. The advent of the consuls was understood by all to be in reality, what it was in name, the inauguration of the Protectorate of Asia Minor ; and it was hailed with joy and relief by almost every section of the population, except the officials. The Consul-General, Sir C. Wilson, was a man who combined the qualifications of knowledge of the East and good judgment ; he was ably seconded, and for a time all went well. Then came a change of government in England and the consuls were no longer supported. The corrupt officials whose degradation they had insisted on were reinstated, and the old state of Turkey was resumed. But the consuls were still in the country, and their presence was an offence to the Porte, a sign of tutelage and subordination, as well as a possible danger in the event of a resumption of active policy in Turkey. The Egyptian War brought an opportunity ; the Sultan gave his authority to Britain to put down the disorder in Egypt,[1] and the consuls

[1] A mere sham, as he was undoubtedly intriguing with Arabi, who represented to the Arabs and Mr. Blunt an anti-Turkish, but to the Turks a Mohammedan movement (*Scotsman*, 25th Sept., 1882).

were ordered away for service in that country. I have often wondered whether the second fact was made a condition of the first—not of course formally, but in an informal way which could be disowned in case of need.

Lord Rosebery, in his Edinburgh speech on 12th Oct., 1896, resigning the leadership of the Liberal party, stated that the military consuls were recalled in 1880, or very shortly after, because they had nothing to do.[1] That is a specimen of the garbled versions of facts about Turkey that our statesmen seem to love. The consuls were not recalled; they were ordered to Egypt on special service in August, 1882. Their power departed when the home government ceased to support them in 1880; but during 1879, they were a great influence in the country; and their presence produced profound and far-reaching results. They were there before the eyes of Moslems and Christians alike, a continual reminder of the overshadowing power of the great Christian kingdom of the West. They were a sign to the people, an omen of the future, " casting out devils " in a literal sense, for where a Mohammedan governor was found by them to be oppressive beyond

---

[1] " Some extra consular officials were appointed in 1879 to supervise any reforms that might be carried out; but in the next year, I think, or very shortly after, they were recalled, I suppose because they had no reforms to supervise."

the average, his deposition followed. Now, the effect produced in Turkey by one or two examples is wonderful; there is nothing like it among the more stubborn and resolute peoples of the West. Thus, the consuls were a beacon of hope to the oppressed and repressed Christians of Eastern Turkey, encouraging them to crave for justice, and fostering in their hearts the inclination to demand the elementary right of personal safety for the person and the family. It was a crime of the deepest dye to plant this hope in the minds of the Armenian Christians, and then to withdraw from the position in which alone we could help them. We formed a partnership, in order to make our partners an excuse for repudiating our old debts.

So far as mere outsiders like me can judge, the Ambassador Extraordinary who was sent to Constantinople with special and unusual powers in May, 1880, Mr. Goschen, must be held more responsible than any other single individual for the change. He was considered to be a man of great influence in his party; and had he understood the case, and resolutely upheld the consuls, he would doubtless have carried the government with him. But the consuls were a creation of the outgoing party; and their success was not likely to be agreeable to the incomers. Moreover, the new government did not wish to be troubled with an active policy in Turkey; it desired to be quit of the whole business as easily as possible, and with the smallest amount of responsibility. So began the wearisome farce of notes presented to the Porte by the six ambassadors of the Great Powers of Europe. But behind the notes there was no strong compelling hand; Britain had resolved not to act; and no one else was likely to do so. British activity was henceforth limited to urging the Powers to present notes; and the Powers were willing to present notes, which meant nothing, and had no more result than occasionally to irritate the Porte, and to keep before its mind the British offence. Meanwhile the Armenians knew that the notes urging on the Porte the necessity of " doing something " in Armenia were due to the insistence of the British ambassadors, and continued to hope that at last Britain would act; but they failed to see that the more they looked to Britain, the more was the face of Russia hardened against them. The Sultan put the notes in the fire, flouted the English in every way, showed special honour to every one whom the British consuls had marked for dishonour, and, naturally, was aided by those Powers whose influence in Turkey grew as British influence waned. No one knew better than the Sultan that the other Great Powers would do nothing against him so long as he was working against England. For my own part, I cannot blame them for making their gain from our loss. The policy of Russia was clear and intelligible throughout, and not any more selfish than ours had been.

In this sketch I have attributed to the Sultan intense religious enthusiasm, patient and far-sighted adaptation of means to gain remote ends, extreme watchfulness, and great powers of work, sufficient to hold in his own hands the direction of the entire course of policy, internal and external—qualities that are as opposite as possible to the Turkish character. Further he has always been greatly averse to inflicting capital punishment on any individual ; now, under the extremely centralised system of administration, no criminal can be executed except under the Sultan's warrant ; and, as this has been almost impossible to procure, he can with perfect justice claim to have abolished capital punishment ; and this has been a fruitful cause of disorder, for the most serious crimes have often gone unpunished. This also is a characteristic most unlike the Turkish nature. Again, the Turks are not a deeply religious race : on the contrary they are as a rule far from assiduous in the cere-monies of the mosque, and readily take any excuse for omitting prayers ; but the Sultan was said to be a member of the Rufai (Howling) Dervishes, and

when the ministers on being summoned to a
council had to wait long, as was often the case,
for the Sultan's appearance, the reason was said by
report to be that he was with a set of Dervishes in
another place waiting till the ecstatic moment had
arrived.   The prophecy used to be current (though
it has long died out in the development of the
Mohammedan revival) that the Empire of Turkey
was to end with an Armenian Sultan, and this was
the Armenian Sultan.   This strange saying was
explained in several ways, some of them too scan-
dalous for belief or quotation ; but the best attested
account was that his mother was an Armenian by
birth, who had adopted Mohammedanism.   This
account, widely believed in 1880-1882, is given as
indubitable in the *North American Review*, Sept.,
1896, p. 280, by Dr. Cyrus Hamlin, who knows
Turkey from thirty-five years' residence as few men
know it.   In more recent years the authorised
statement is that the Sultan's mother was a Georgian
or Circassian—people vary as to the exact race.
The important point is that every one recognises
how essentially unlike Turkish is the Sultan's
character ; and every one feels that the explanation lies in the inheritance from his mother.
For my own part, the Armenian origin seems to
me proved by the results : only Armenian parent-
age gives the clue to the Sultan's character, his

unwearied carefulness, his prevision, his personal timidity (which keeps him always a prisoner within his own palace walls), his fear of the Turks, his hatred for the Armenians, and the other qualities already described.

This man, who has played the part of Mithridates in the nineteenth century and played it with such skill and success, with scheming head, not with warlike hands, well deserves the historian's study. It is a remarkable part that he has undertaken, to stem the tide of change, which the three previous Sultans accepted as inevitable, and to stifle the growth of civilisation in Turkey, which the strongest party in Turkey desired. The task would have been impossible, had it not been for the resources that civilisation put in his hands; for, indubitably, modern inventiveness, by facilitating destruction, places enormous power in the hands of barbarism. His ally, without whom he could not have done nearly so much, has been Germany. It was patent to every one as far back as 1882 that the Sultan, feeling he had nothing to fear from German aggression, inclined to favour that country, which became immensely influential in Constantinople and has remained so ever since. Each party had much to gain: neither had anything to lose. German capital found an opening in Turkish enterprises; German officers organised the Turkish army; Krupp supplied the guns, and Germans calculated the range, did all the more scientific part of artillery practice, and taught the soldiers to do the simpler work. The Sultan wanted an effective army to defend his life and to crush disaffection; and the Germans gave it to him. So long as German officers are there to guide the operations, and so long as they succeed in keeping the supreme command out of the hands of some incapable Turk (like the "hero of Plevna," [1] who sat behind his lines, smoked, and ate, until the Russians overcame his stubborn soldiers) and in the hands of some good Mohammedan officer, the Sultan can do as he will in the East. German railways radiate from the Bosphorus over Asia Minor. German enterprises get every facility they require. People may blame the selfish policy of Germany; but her policy has been no more selfish than that of every other European power interested in the East, our own included.

The history of the "Eastern Question" is always the same. It is always to the interest of one or two of the European Powers to support Turkey against the rest; and thus the Porte subsists on the divisions among the Christians. For a long time it was thought conducive to "British interests" to support Turkey, and we did so consistently and

---

[1] Known as the greatest "eater" (*i.e.*, of bribes) in Turkey.

persistently. At the present time it is the interest of Russia and Germany to support Turkey: Russia knows that the Sultan has for many years been steadily undermining British influence in Turkey, Germany finds that it gains many advantages from the informal alliance. The "Confederacy of Europe," while pretending to exist for the maintenance of order in Turkey, works entirely for the advantage of Germany and Russia, which happen for the moment to be identical; and the form under which the whole is worked is that the preservation of the "Concert" is the only way of avoiding a European war. Undoubtedly, Russia and Germany would not without war submit to any action that they would regard as tending to re-invigorate the waning moral power of Britain in Turkey. The Armenian movement always aspired towards the freedom of America and Britain, not towards the autocracy of Russia; and therefore the Armenians must suffer. Russia has learned that the educated Eastern Christians, even if freed by her armies and bound by gratitude to her, as the Bulgarians were, do not love her rule; much less will she permit that the Armenians should be saved in a way that they would attribute to English support. Now it is plain to every one who reads the official correspondence with any understanding of the situation, that the proposed action on behalf of the

Armenians was from the first always of such a character as would be most certain to strengthen Armenian gratitude towards England, and tend to make the Armenian people a bar against the development of Russian influence along the south coast of the Black Sea. This is not a question merely of the last two or three years ; it entered on the present phase when a Liberal government came into power in April, 1880, and proceeded to reverse our whole action in Turkey, abandoning our strong position, and throwing away our advantages. In order to shirk responsibility, they began to hide behind the " Concert of Europe," hoping that the other Powers would act with them ; but the majority had everything to gain by thwarting us, and they naturally declined to play our game. Thus Britain gave Russia and Turkey the opportunity which they were eager to use, and opened the way for the great development of German influence, which has been the most striking feature in my experience of Turkish life. British statesmen have had a very difficult part to play in the last three years, since the question reached its acutest stage, and they have played it with uniform ill-success. But it is certain that nothing is gained by keeping up the sham which is at present maintained before our country; and the beginning of any better state of things in Turkey will not be made, till it comes to be a rule among our rulers first to understand, and then to tell the truth about, the Eastern bungle. I often have wondered, in reading the utterances of officials in both parties, whether the managers of our Eastern policy are selected because of their skill in misrepresenting, or their power of misunderstanding, Turkish affairs. Sometimes the one theory seems more natural, sometimes the other.

It may be said for the former English policy that, in general, it supported and encouraged the best elements in Turkish life. It was too blind to the inevitable predominance of the worst elements in the government, and often too weak in checking them, when it was not blind to them. But, except in the one damning case of the Bulgarian massacres, no British Government deliberately and consciously championed the worst side of Turkish action ; and it must be allowed that those massacres sprang more from the weakness of the Porte and its utter inability to control the elemental forces of barbarism within the Empire, than from any deliberate plan. Our statesmen had a vague belief that Turkey might be reformed with care and time ; and they hoped on with foolish, but well-meant, credulity. But, at the present day, the European Concert is supporting the worst elements in Turkey ; and, perhaps, our co-operation in a policy which is planned for the benefit of Russia and Germany is a just punishment for the crime of supporting the Bulgarian massacres, and the duplicity of the Cyprus Convention.

Will the Sultan's policy be successful? Will the revival of Mohammedanism be permanent in Asia Minor? So far as the centre and west is concerned, it cannot be. The Moslems are dying out there. Even where the Greeks have not begun to settle, the Turks are diminishing in numbers owing to conscription, misgovernment, and moral causes, on which I will not enter, because I have avoided studying or observing them. They have no heart. They are in the grip of the railways, and under the influence of Europe. In the eastern regions it may be different for a time. The Mohammedan revival has been far more carefully propagated in those lands, and for the moment it is successful by the usual Turkish method. As it was in Scio in 1821 and in Syria in 1860, so it is there at the present time, but on a vastly greater scale,—the signs of western spirit, western education and aspirations after the elementary rights of freedom alarmed the Turks, and they have set to work, after long preparation and on a carefully deliberated plan, to crush the hostile western spirit by general and indiscriminate massacre. The Armenians will in all probability be exterminated, except the remnant that escapes to other lands. There can be little doubt that about 200,000 of them have been actually put to death by the Turks, and I believe that fully four times as many have either died of starvation and hardship, or have so suffered from the unspeakable brutality to which they have been subjected, that they can never again be self-respecting men and women.

At present, in the western regions of Asia Minor, the feeling is almost universal that the Mohammedan revival in the east will, when it has done its work there, be extended also to the west. The Greeks are a far greater danger to the Turks than the Armenians ever were. They have been less submissive, more audacious, more inclined to revolt, more successful in asserting themselves against the Turks. They will not long escape, when the Armenians are exterminated and Orientalism is once more supreme in the east, and they recognise this; and no rational man, who judges of others from a fair point of view, can blame them if they attempt to forestall the fate intended for them.

But even in the eastern parts of Asia Minor the Oriental spirit is doomed. The Kurds will massacre as many Armenians as the Porte wishes, but they will never be good Mohammedans or subjects of the Sultan, except in outward show. It remains to be seen whether they are capable of being reduced to order by the stern discipline of a western government; they can never be controlled by the Turkish officials, feeble in everything except a massacre. Most of us, probably, will live to see the boundary between European and Asiatic rule placed near the Euphrates.

We shall wholly misconceive the present state of things in Asia Minor, unless we bear in mind the facts which have been stated in the preceding paragraphs. The situation in Turkey is not simply an uneasy balance between two opposite forces, where a little extra strength added to one side by the European Powers can restore equilibrium. Orientalism is ebbing and dying in the country. The tide of western ideas and western thoughts is flowing and strong; eight centuries of strict and stern repression are behind it and drive it onward irresistibly. The Great Powers of Europe, as they feebly and nervelessly protest against the movement towards freedom, and officially disown it, and stand for the constituted authority and rights of the Sultan, and reprobate the undue haste of Armenians and Cretans and the Young Turkish party to free themselves from the incubus that crushes them, are in the position of Canute when he set bounds to the flowing tide. The world, the course of history, and the mind of man, are against the Powers; and there is nothing possible for them in the long run except an ignominious retreat from their position, amid the contempt and the reprobation of mankind, whose feelings they are now outraging. They are now abusing the resources of civilised society and government, to support and prop up the feeblest and most contemptible administration by which barbarism and organised disorder ever tried to stifle enlightenment and order. But they cannot do more, they do not even pretend to do more, than prolong its dying agonies a few months or years ; they do not think, and they hardly plead as an excuse, that they are lessening the inevitable dangers of its dissolution by postponement ; some of them, doubtless, know (as those of my acquaintance, that are most familiar with the East, all feel) that they are only increasing those dangers by staving them off for the moment. They can drill a good army for the Sultan, and Turks are very good material for soldiers ; but they cannot put permanent vitality into the Asiatic reaction.

The thing which they can and will succeed in doing is that they destroy the moderate and orderly element in the new movement ; for the sober, intelligent, and reasonable men among the Armenians, those who have borne the toil and danger of patiently, quietly educating the people in the ways of peace, are far most exposed to massacre, and have been specially marked out in every case for the revenge of the brutal mob and more brutal officials, while the harebrained revolutionists, maddened by suspense and overhanging fear of massacre, who seized the Ottoman Bank in Constantinople, are the class which generally escapes, and becomes more reckless and inflamed.

But we have spoken only of the six European Powers. What about America? As is stated on pp. 222, 227, the factor that has been most potent in producing the movement towards freedom has been the American educational organisation. What attitude does the American Government assume towards this organisation, and towards the Power which threatens and longs for and works for its destruction? Many Americans, unconnected with the missionaries, whom I have met, have said that the American Government was likely to have great influence with the Porte, because it could be trusted to have no designs in Turkey. Those who spoke thus had always, as I found, been in communication with the American Ministry at Constantinople; and their exact agreement in view seemed to me to reflect the impression which they, as strangers, derived from the official view held at the Ministry. This view ignores entirely the whole work of the missionaries ; and I am under the impression that officials in America (who, of course, reflect the ideas entertained at the Ministry in

Constantinople) are almost entirely ignorant of the real character and power and guaranteed rights of the American educational equipment in Turkey. It may seem extraordinary that the great machinery of colleges and schools which the missionaries have created should be so completely ignored, as it is in the very statement of this view ; but the official mind has an extraordinary power of ignoring anything that is not official, and the missionaries' work, being a missionary and unselfish work, is despised by many as of no account in practical life. The Sultan's Government, however, is not blind to it, and would gladly destroy it, and pull down every college and school ; but a long series of recognitions and authorisations from the three Sultans stand in the way. The pretence that the Porte may regard the American Government as specially friendly, because their interests can never conflict, is used as a means of managing the Minister ; and has always hitherto been entirely successful. But, besides the missionary stumbling-block, the Americans can offer no return to the Sultan ; they could do him no service except to remove the missionaries ; they cannot drill his armies, or give him any of the practical aid and the moral support that lies in the friendship of a commander of vast armies in Europe, which the German Emperor can give. And, as the Sultan has nothing to gain from the Americans, he has never granted them even one of the stones which they excavated at Assos.

Much as the American politicians may dislike it, there is no doubt that the interest and influence among others of both English-speaking races are closely connected. Zealously as the missionaries have tried to be non-political, their work has told, and must tell, strongly in favour of the free civilisation of the English-speaking races, and against the bureaucratic civilisation of Russia or Germany. American official influence can be great in Turkey only when it is exerted on the side of freedom and in maintenance of the rights of the existing American enterprises ; but for a time it has been directed towards the other side, and consequently it has been null. We can only wait and hope for better counsels.

Russian policy has been clear and consistent throughout ; and in agreement with Russia against German influence in Turkey lies our only rational course. But that course is not likely to be taken, till Lord Salisbury has given place to a successor (p. 144).

CHAPTER VII.

GOVERNMENT AND OFFICIALS.

IT cannot be too emphatically stated that the evil in Turkey does not arise from bad laws. The laws are, taking them as a whole, good, being as a rule adapted by Mahmud or his successors from the most approved European legislation. The entire theory laid down by the reforming Sultans as to the relations between the various religions of the country is fair and generous. The whole procedure that is prescribed in cases of conversion to Mohammedanism from any other form of religion is judicious, moderate, and calculated to distinguish between real and enforced conversion, and to give the former co-religionists of the convert every opportunity of satisfying themselves that the conversion is voluntary. The evil lies in the administration of the laws. All the best part of the law, one might almost say the whole of the modern law, is a dead letter, except where there happens to be a vigorous and hard-working consul, familiar with Eastern manners and language, backed by an experienced and judicious ambassador, and actively supported by his home government ; and where is that the case? Instances of it I have, however, known, and the good achieved I have seen for myself.

Among the Turkish officials, however, there is, in the first place, rarely any desire to carry out the law, any knowledge of what the law provides, or any wish to learn what are the provisions of the law. The aim of the official in Turkey is not to know and carry into effect the law. The existing practice would make it impossible for him to execute it, and no one can say that he ought to try to know what he cannot execute, especially as it would mean ruin to himself. And, in the second place, the salaries apportioned to officials are absurdly small. I remember in one case the governor of a district as large as Yorkshire had a salary of £T. 70 per annum. Moreover, the salary is generally hopelessly in arrears. Finally, the official has often to pay in bribes, before he gets his appointment, much more than it is worth. In order to live he must do as his neighbours do ; bribery is the universal rule ; everything everywhere moves by *bakshish*, and without it nothing can be done. The duty of an official is not to carry out the law, but to meet the expenses of life. He has his appointment ; he knows that it won't last long, for changes are frequent, and he must make the best of his time.   Everybody knows what the system is ; no one expects him to do otherwise ; nobody blames him for doing as all know that they would do in the same circumstances.   It is difficult to see what improvement is possible until there is a reform at the heart.

Moreover, the Turk is not naturally a good officer or a good official.   In the first place he is indolent, and incapable of voluntarily undertaking the active life of a vigorous officer.   The idea is deep in his nature that the object of life is to make money in order that he may sit still the whole day long.   Why be an official and a great man, if he has to work as hard as a poor man?   He is capable of making an exertion under the stimulus of poverty ; and I have it on the best authority that a set of Turkish navvies are second to none as good and useful workmen (but doubtless this excellence depends on the tact of the organising superintendent).   He makes an excellent soldier, hardy, well-behaved under discipline, who can be trusted to fight till he is cut to pieces, both behind fortified lines and in the open field ; but he must have officers to lead him, and he seems hardly ever capable of taking on education enough for an officer. When the stimulus of compulsion from above is removed, he sits down, and lets things slide.   Even among a set of workmen you must employ overseers of a different race ; the same Turk who is excellent as a workman is useless as an overseer, while you will get lots of Greeks who make useful overseers but bad manual labourers. The hewers of wood, the carriers of stones, and that class of workmen in general on the railways are Turks (so far as my experience goes), but the employees of higher class are to a large extent Greeks. It is difficult, perhaps impossible, to educate the Turk ; but there are so many sterling qualities in him, that I have a profound conviction that he can be amalgamated with other elements to form a good mixed race.

As an official, then, the Turk is dependent on educated help to enable him to perform his duties : usually he does not trouble to read for himself papers presented to him, but has them read to him:[1] often one has a strong suspicion, sometimes positive certainty, that reading would be so difficult to the official that he cannot trust himself to get the meaning of the document. My experience is that any Turkish official, who can read documents with ease and understanding, makes a point of doing so in public, in order to impress his inferior officers and the general population. You will occasionally be told, as a matter worth note, that such and such

---

[1] I speak only of what I have seen, which is chiefly in the inner country, not in Stambol or Smyrna.

an official can read any paper presented to him ; and the reputation produces so much effect on everybody, that it must be rare. The Turks cannot go through the elementary and indispensable routine of government without the aid of a great number of Christian subalterns. That has always been the case ; they have always found plenty of Armenians and Phanariote Greeks to serve them in this capacity ; and the most tyrannous and oppressive officials in grinding into the dust the Bosnian and Herzegovinian Christians were these Greeks (as Mr. Arthur Evans,[1] a staunch champion of the Christians of Turkey, emphatically states). It is said that the present Sultan, when he came into power, began by attempting to make a clean sweep of all Armenian employees in government service.[2] Success was of course impossible, for Turkish officials to take their place could not be found ; and hence the Sultan was able recently (as the newspapers mentioned) to retort on those who accused him of hating the Armenians, that he had in his official service in Stambol so many hundreds of Armenians.

But it is useless to import a cartload of good laws into a country, if no provision is made to

---

[1] *Through Bosnia and Herzegovina*, p. 257.

[2] See Dr. Cyrus Hamlin, in *North American Review*, Sept., 1896, p. 280.

train a set of officials, competent to carry them
into effect. No machinery exists sufficient to train
the officials, or to ensure that a class exists educated
enough to appreciate a complicated system of law
and the complicated procedure needed to give
effect to it. I have known a few vigorous and
intelligent officials in Turkey, but as a rule their
activity was directed to carry out a plain and simple
style of administration of the semi-patriarchal type,
where a rough sense of justice took the place of
knowledge of the law, and filled that place quite
satisfactorily amid a simple and elementary form
of society. Why then—the question is sure to be
put—is it said that good officials cannot be made
out of Turks? Is not my experience sufficient to
show that active and intelligent officials do exist
among them, and can be found and trained when
wanted? But in most cases where I have found
such an official, I have also been told that he was
not a Turk, but an Albanian, or occasionally a
Circassian, or so on. The very Turks who were
my informants themselves recognised the strange-
ness of active business-like character in a Turk, and
unasked explained the reason.

The want of proper training for boys already
spoken of,[1] is apparent, when the attempt is made
to train the young men into officers. Leave an

[1] See pp. 43, 49, 270.

English boy to grow up among servants and grooms and lackeys (even though these are highly educated men compared to the great mass of Turks), without giving him any proper intellectual or moral education, and the result would be unpromising. Some attempt was made by the reforming Sultans to create a system of schools; but, like everything Turkish, the thing has been a failure.

Reform and improvement, in short, are quite possible in Turkey, but not under Turkish rule. As the author of *Anadol* said of the Ottoman Government, " bodies politic, like those of men, require a certain degree of soul to keep them from becoming carrion ; to save the expense of salt, as old Ben Jonson says ". The longer you travel in Turkey, the more profoundly do you become convinced, like the traveller from whom I quote, that the administration is devoid of the requisite " degree of soul ". As Hamilton puts it, " every one must feel that the Turks themselves are as yet incapable of that high moral energy and perseverance in the path of duty, which are essential to the accomplishment of any moral or political regeneration " (*Researches*, i., p. 355).

The mingled hatred and fear with which the Turkish peasantry regard the officials of the government is more deep seated and far reaching in its effects than one would readily believe. On one occasion in 1890, when the only possible means of getting photographs and impressions of an important " Hittite " relief with inscription at Bor (which I have long been in pursuit of) was to purchase it, and present it to the Imperial Museum in Constantinople, lodging it for the moment under the care of the government, this act proved afterwards a serious impediment to our chances of further discovery. Having once been guilty of trafficking with government, by giving to it what we had purchased from a too confiding private vendor, we had made ourselves agents of the officials, and (as I doubt not) had become the means whereby the previous owner lost both the stone and the price. Parts of the tale have been told in his own effective style by my friend, the " Wandering Scholar " (see his p. 14 ff.), and I need not here retell it more fully ; but there are some gaps in his narrative which his literary skill disguises ; and, as an unintended result, there remains in the reader's mind an erroneous conception, that the distrust entertained by every one for government agents was a mere freak of ignorant bigotry. It was the experience of many years which produced that distrust. In ordinary circumstances, as soon as it came to the knowledge of government that the Greek woman from whom we bought the stone had received twenty pounds for it, an agent would visit her and extort from her the largest part of the money; and she might be thankful, if by sacrificing the part voluntarily she could purchase leave to keep the remainder. There have been many cases in which, on the bare suspicion of having come into possession of money, people have been subjected to imprisonment and torture from sheer inability to pay up more than they really had received.

Whether the Greek woman actually had to pay hush money to the officials I am not in a position to state positively, but I thought so soon after, and still think so. And if she got off easily and cheaply, what was the reason? It was simply that fear of European opinion has greatly weakened the once heavy hand of the Turk in the western and central parts of Asiatic Turkey. The sympathy that unites all the Greeks in self-defence has given them comparative safety, and makes an official slow to rouse them and fairly easy to bribe.

Not that it has been only the Christians who suffered in this way. Far from it; and I take the proof from this same incident. The "Wandering Scholar" was led secretly and at midnight by devious ways into a garden which he knew not, where the precious second half of the relief was offered him by a man whose name he did not learn, and whom he had never seen, provided that "he pledged himself solemnly to have no dealings with the government in the matter ". That man, who was so eager to get rid of "this dangerous thing, which robbed him of sleep," was himself a Turk,[1] belonging to the richest private family in the district. But he was even more distrustful of the government than the Greeks had been. Either the Greeks had been emboldened formerly by the banded support which all Greeks give one another, whereas Turks never aid any one, but accept the decrees of God and the stroke of fate unresistingly, or the owner of the second half of the relief had been warned by the fate of the Greek owner of the first half.

The longest chapter of this book might be devoted to giving examples of the oppressive and blind way in which government is administered. But every traveller who has been long enough in Turkey to acquire any knowledge of its ways, is

[1] I think I mentioned his name in a letter in the *Athenæum* at the time. I spent a night in the house of his brother (who is described above, p. 22) at Tyana, and heard from him of the stone in his brother's possession. Being compelled to hurry away to catch the steamer at Mersina, I could not accept his invitation to go with him next morning to see the stone. The " Wandering Scholar " had arranged to meet me the following evening near the Cilician Gates, and I intended to instruct him how to reach the stone (which was a delicate matter), but he was prevented from completing the journey in time, and I could only leave a brief message and hurry on.

full of them; and the inquiring reader may find some good and characteristic stories in Mr. Barkley's *Ride through Asia Minor*. The point which I wish to emphasise is that, previous to the recent massacres, and excluding what may be called "the black country" (in which the Armenians have been long exposed to continual suffering from the Kurds), it was the Mohammedan peasantry who on the whole seemed to me to suffer most from the perversity and iniquity of government. The Christians, even in the villages (I speak here only of Central and Western Anatolia) were richer and cleverer than the Mohammedans; and they could better avail themselves of those ways by which matters can be made easy with the officials. One who lives much among the Moslem peasantry, and sympathises with them, as I have done, comes to hate the Ottoman government with that fervent hatred which I feel.

The subordinate agents of the government, who come most in contact with the peasant population, are the *Zaptiehs* or *gens d'armes*. I have not the knowledge requisite to give an accurate, complete account of the character of these Turkish police; and it is not the aim of this little book to do more than set forth the impression made on me by what I have seen and heard. The action of the *Zaptiehs*, of course, varies according to the character of the governor ; and in Turkey there have been in my experience some good governors, such as Ingleez Said in Konia, kept there for many years in an honourable sort of exile, Abeddin Pasha, and various others. The influence of these men kept their provinces in a much better condition than the average ; and Said's officials were positively paid their salaries regularly, or at least it was so represented to him. But it was also formally reported to him that the great road through the Cilician Gates was finished to the extreme limit of his government ;[1] and I can certify that all the easy parts of the road were finished properly, only some of the bridges were unbuilt, so that the causeway could not be used for a stretch of miles, and the most difficult part of the road within the Konia government had been left in its natural condition, on the principle that it was too bad to improve. It is true that the light country waggon (*araba*) could be driven over the whole road ; but the " Wandering Scholar " and I (who have taken a waggon up the ridge of Anti-Taurus, where no path had ever gone, and lowered it by a rope down the other side) don't think that that implies a very high character for the road. Even Said Pasha, then, could not do everything ; but he did

[1] Conversing with us in 1882, he spoke with some pride of having completed this road up to the limit of his authority.

a good deal, and his *Zaptiehs* were not the average Turkish policemen.

But I want to show what the peasants think about the *Zaptiehs*, and to give some examples of the reason why they think as they do. Your average *Zaptieh* gets no pay, for his nominal salary (like that of most officials, especially the humbler class) is so hopelessly in arrears that we may fairly say he gets none. Even a *Zaptieh* must live and support his family, and in the country districts he must provide and keep his horse. His country is bound to do that; and as she does not do it in the regular way, he must make his livelihood out of the peasantry in irregular fashion. He lives, of course, free, and behaves as a sufficiently brutal lord and master wherever he goes among the peaceful and submissive Turks, though he finds it wise to keep a quieter tongue in his head when he has to go among Circassians or Kurds or Avshahrs. He has the task of communicating orders from the government to the villages, where the headman receives the instructions. If the taxes are not paid, the *Zaptiehs* have to inquire the reason why, and make the headman recognise the necessities of the case; and the archæologist, as he sits in the Oda, may, if he likes, hear many a tale of oppression and cruelty.

To our sophisticated Western minds, a policeman is a symbol of law, and his chief duty is to arrest and imprison the criminal, and protect the industrious citizen. A *Zaptieh's* view is very different. If a crime has been committed, his business is to wink at the criminal, to arrest the neighbours in succession, and to put them in prison, until they have made it worth his while to let them out. If he arrested the criminal, his trade would be ruined. In a large town, where I have been a good deal, a murder was committed some years ago : an elderly Turk was found dead in his own house. Everybody knew who was the murderer. It was the Turk's own son-in-law, who was tired of waiting for his death to enter on the inheritance of his wife. The old man's head had been cut off, which was a sure proof that a Turkish hand had been at work. The Turk, when he kills, always cuts off the head : even the fowl for your archæologist's soup is slaughtered by decapitation. On the contrary, the Greek race has never been given to mutilation of the human form ; it is true that the Smyrniote blackguards are much addicted to the use of the knife, and murders are frequent among them ; but they are satisfied with simple murder, and leave the corpse entire. But in this case most of the Greeks in the neighbourhood were arrested, imprisoned, and set free in the usual style ; and, when I passed that way four months after the murder, not a Turk had yet been arrested, while the well-known culprit was enjoying his inheritance. After all, what difference did it make? There are no habitual criminals in Turkey, and no criminal class. The same man is a respectable tradesman one day, and has taken to the hills the next—to return to his trade after a decent interval. The Turk in this case had no other father-in-law, and was not likely to commit another murder. Why should your *Zaptieh* trouble him about this one peccadillo?

Whatever be the case in the best administered districts and among individuals, the fact is that the *Zaptiehs* are associated in the minds of the people generally with every act of oppression and extortion that takes place. If you ask about any act of brigandage on the great trade road between Angora and Constantinople (I speak of days before the railway ran to Angora), you will hear that it was all arranged in collusion with the authorities, and the *Zaptiehs* who acted as intermediaries will probably be named. If you inquire into the antecedents of the redoubtable Osman, who was keeping the Konia country· lively for some years before 1890, a tale of hard and unfair treatment will be unfolded to you, in which Osman is the suffering hero and *Zaptiehs* the tormentors. If you get your servant, *e.g.*, one whom I employed in 1887, a tall, thin, cadaverous-looking Turk, to tell you the history of his eleven years' imprisonment, he connects all his sufferings, beginning with his unjust arrest in his seventeenth year, with the *Zaptiehs*; and he declares that the *Zaptiehs* took bribes from the real culprit to charge the crime on an innocent powerless poor man. If you hear one of the American missionaries give evidence of the way in which the headman of an Armenian village, which had been raided and looted by Kurds, was tortured to death in his own house for declaring his inability to raise the usual amount of tax, and persisting after due warning in this rebellious declaration, it was the *Zaptiehs* who put a chain round his waist, passed it over a beam in the roof, and hauled the wretched man up and let him down again, until the chain cut into him, and he died of the treatment. In the country districts, when you hear of ill-will between the Christian villages and the Moslem, it is rarely, if ever, so far as my experience goes, a direct hatred against the hostile village: it is mediated through the *Zaptiehs* or even still higher officials, who are declared on the one side to take bribes from the wealthier Christians and let them off their fair taxation, and on the other side to allow the Moslem villages, from religious partiality, to be a year or two in arrears.

I do not give these instances as being either all

verified truth,[1] or as a complete and fair judgment; but every one of them embodies a statement which I have listened to and sympathised with; I could quote many more stories of similar type; I cannot quote a single testimony, or observation on my own part, of good feeling and kindly relations between villagers and *Zaptiehs*. I have found everywhere and among all kinds of the Anatolian people and all religions the same belief—that the police of Turkey are the centre and agents of disorder, misgovernment, and injustice.

That being the case, whether rightly or wrongly, what was likely to be the effect of the orders issued in Crete by the six Great Powers—orders (in Lord Salisbury's own words) that, after the Greek troops were required to retire, the Turkish troops should for the present be retained to police the island under the proposed system of autonomy?

To keep up Turkish police was to destroy any chance of the proffered autonomy being accepted, for it was received as an intimation that the worst evils were to be maintained and supported by the Great Powers. Every man who knows Turkey recognised that the retention of the Turks as police was either an absurdity, the result of ignorance,

---

[1] Except when it comes from an American missionary or a consul; but of them there are so many, that the rest are not needed to strengthen the case.

which destroyed any benefit in the other arrangements, or an intentional device to maintain the Sultan's authority in spite of illusory promises made to hoodwink the Greeks. While it would, beyond a doubt, have been the duty of the Greek government and troops to accept the autonomy professedly offered by the Great Powers and to retire, if the Turkish troops had all been obliged to evacuate the island (either immediately or before some definite day), and only European soldiers and sailors employed to keep order, it was equally their duty to persist and to fight to the end, so long as Turkish soldiers remained in the island. To withdraw and leave the Turks as guardians of order would have been to advertise themselves as either braggart cowards, who had begun a work and stopped when they found it to be dangerous, or fools who, after centuries of experience, could still accept an assurance that the Turks would maintain peace and order. It is a reasonable view to hold that the Greeks should not have gone into Crete at all; and I am not prepared to hold that it was wise, nor would I have said one word to encourage them, if I had been in a position to speak, knowing their weakness and want of preparation and M. Deliyanni's ridiculous incompetence. But it is an irrational thing to maintain that they ought to have retired, when autonomy and Turkish police were offered.   After once going there, it was inconsistent with self-respect to withdraw, until something more than absurdity or cheat was proffered them.

Personally, I have no reason to dislike the *Zaptiehs*.   To myself, certainly, they were always most obedient, respectful, and obliging ; several of them were intelligent and really useful, and all were willing and zealous ; but I had the power of the purse, and they all knew my reputation as paying well for services, and paying nothing but hard words or worse for idleness and failure.   But, as a rule, I avoided employing *Zaptiehs*, and rarely took them, except when they were pressed upon me by Pashas and other high officials.   They were, of course, intended to be spies and checks upon me ; but that was not the reason why it was best to avoid them, for I had no wish to do anything illegal and nothing to conceal ; while, as to vexatious interference, a judicious hint at the beginning about *bakshish* arranges such matters easily in Turkey.   The real objection to the presence of a *Zaptieh* was that he was distrusted and suspected by the villagers, and was therefore an impediment to discovery ; and in several cases I knew, and in others thought, that payment made to villagers for showing inscriptions was seized by a *Zaptieh*, or at least a heavy percentage was levied by him on it.

It is familiar to every resident in Smyrna that,

when some serious crime rouses public indignation, private citizens must track it out and insist on punishment, if anything is to be done. For example, about eighteen years ago, two Montenegrins, who had been dismissed from the service of a Levantine family residing near Smyrna, in revenge for the slight put upon them, attacked the house by night, murdered one member of the family, and left three others lying half dead. If the matter had been left to the officials, many arrests would have been made ; but the Montenegrins would probably have lived on unharmed. The European community, however, resolved that such a deed should not pass unpunished. Every one knew who the murderers were ; but they had to be found, and they had to be arrested. Now Montenegrins are always men of great courage and personal strength ; and to arrest two desperate, well-armed, powerful men is no easy matter. They were followed up and caught by the man, whose name rises to the lips of every person in the whole country round, not English only, but of many nationalities, when any action is required for the public welfare, demanding courage, coolness, and knowledge of the country— Mr. Richard Whittall—in whose office the murdered man had been a clerk. Taking with him a single Turkish servant, he tracked them to a room in Smyrna, and delivered them over to the police.

They were tried and found guilty ; and it was, I think, finally arranged that they met their death at the hands of justice—not an easy thing to accomplish in Turkey.

As to the matter of public order, things vary much. The trade roads are often unsafe, and the western coast lands are generally more or less infested by brigands. Wherever there is any money to be picked up by robbing or brigandage, that trade is well kept up. But over a considerable part of the central country, poverty is so universal, that there is hardly anything for a robber to live by, and his trade languishes. You hear many stories of robbers and loose characters about the country, as you wander, and on rare occasions you learn that the head of a robber is exposed at the Konak (government house) of a city. I have occasionally met a set of *Zaptiehs*, who were out in pursuit of a band of robbers ; but the only thing they sometimes succeed in doing is to arrest and imprison the family of a man they are in search of. For example, in 1884, we were told of a band consisting of three Circassians and two Yuruks, who were roaming the Phrygian mountains, and defying the police. One day, we met half a dozen *Zaptiehs*, and were informed that they had seized the whole family of one of the two Yuruks, and sent them in charge to Kutaya.

As a general rule you need not pay any attention to reports of this kind. The only logical conclusion, if you paid any attention, would be that you should go away from the district. But such parties rarely molest Europeans ; and you may feel comparatively safe if you do not neglect the ordinary dictates of prudence. I heard of one party on an excursion who were riding in several waggons. They had to ascend a long slope, up which the horses walked ; and, as is usual in such cases, the waggons became separated by considerable intervals. Each waggon, on reaching the top, instead of waiting for the stragglers to close up, dashed down the hill at a rapid pace, and widened the interval still more. Some Circassians on the lookout waited until the last waggon came up to the top of the hill separated by a long distance from the rest, overturned it by the roadside, stripped the inmates of everything they possessed worth taking, and left them free to make up on their flying predecessors and tell their experiences. A party should never travel in this straggling order ; but it is hardly conceivable how difficult it is to induce undisciplined and careless travellers to observe this elementary rule.

I was also told of another case in which a European and his servant, sleeping under a tree, were murdered and robbed by some Circassians.

On two occasions when we had been camping

for some days in the open country, report or the suspicious appearance and questions of a Circassian made me think it prudent to flit at a moment's notice to a village. And, as a general rule, one should not stay for more than one night in any place except a village, though I must plead guilty to having several times violated this rule. For a single night, except with bad luck, you are not likely to see or be seen by any one, if you camp out in the open country.

It is also a principle not to be too open in telling your plans of travel, especially when you are travelling in a small party. You naturally question everybody about the roads, the course of the water, the distance of various towns, the list of villages on the way to them, and so on. As you will yourself see the road which you intend to travel, you need not ask much about it; and the natives conclude that you are going any way except the road about which you show no curiosity. When you meet a small party of riders you should not ask them the distance and direction of the place to which you are going, but be vague and general in your conversation, otherwise you may regret it.

Though I have often heard reports about lurking dangers, I never actually found myself in an obviously dangerous position, except perhaps on the following occasion, and even that is a matter of circumstantial evidence and therefore uncertain.

In August, 1883, I was going across the great treeless plain which stretches west and south from the upper Sangarios : with me there was one Bosniak Turk, Murad. We were due to reach a bridge over the river Sangarios after a two hours' ride ; but at the end of two hours we seemed as far away as ever from the river, and had evidently missed our road. At this moment, over the brow of a low slope in front of us appeared three mounted Circassians. I felt much relieved, as Circassians have always wonderful knowledge of country and direction ; but, to my annoyance, Murad, who was about ten yards in front, did not stop to ask them the way. I was on the point of stopping myself, but by some chance or caprice, did not do so. I quickened my pace and asked Murad why he had not asked the way, as we were obviously wrong. He said, " These men are robbers ". As I knew the feeling that all Turks entertain towards Circassians, I ridiculed the idea ; but he pointed back over his shoulder, declaring that Circassians had no business here, more than fourteen hours from their nearest village ; and as I glanced back I saw that they were standing, turning towards us and talking. At this moment we crossed the brow of the slope, passed out of their sight, and came on a solitary threshing floor, where a number of men and women were gathering in the produce of some fields. They told us they belonged to a village at the bridge towards which we were bound, that we were going in the wrong direction, and must turn sharp off to the left, *i.e.*, the north, in order to reach the bridge, which was full two hours distant. We went according to their directions; and, as Murad expressed great uneasiness about the Circassians, and we were so late, we quickened our pace, and went as fast as his horse, a very poor one, could be made to go. We came to several forks in the road, and made a shot at hazard as to the proper path. About fifty minutes had passed when Murad said, "There are the Circassians". Sure enough the same three men were visible, not a very great distance away, and riding rapidly towards us. They were now on the opposite side. We had left them riding away from us towards the west, but they were now coming up towards us from the south-east. The only possible explanation seemed to be that they, knowing about the threshing floor and not venturing to turn back after us past the people there, had made a circuit by the south, intending to attack us on the other side of the threshing floor out of sight of the people. Our sudden turn away on a new road had disconcerted them; and they had lost some time, before they found out where we had gone.   Naturally we did our best to get on; but they were much better mounted, and gained on us rapidly.   My only weapons were sundry surveying instruments. Murad had an American breech-loading hunting rifle, with a delicate fixed sight, not intended to shoot beyond 200 yards, but deadly up to that range.   But he was not a practised shot : in fact, Turks as a rule are bad shots; and he was obviously so excited, that it was doubtful if he could have hit a haystack.   I resolved that, if I got out of this business, I should learn to use a rifle.   Two of the Circassians, as I noticed in passing, had only old flint-lock guns, and the third one of the common muzzle-loading, double-barrelled fowling pieces, which are sold all over Turkey very cheap, and generally very bad, of Belgian make; but all three had large revolvers, and the usual armoury of weapons at their waists.   Had Prof. Sterrett, to whom our rifle belonged, been with us, we should have been easier, as he was a dead shot and not given to excitement ; but we could only hope that the Circassians were the victims of deceitful appearance, and that the bridge was near.   Just at that moment the bridge appeared to our longing eyes ; the Circassians stopped short about 200 yards behind us ; and we saw them no more.   But at the bridge the villagers said that the three had been prowling about the neighbourhood for a week, and had lifted a few things here and there. This was the nearest approach I ever had to an interview with robbers; and, after all, as I said before, there is only uncertain circumstantial evidence against our Circassian friends.

CHAPTER VIII.

THE ARMENIANS.

THROUGHOUT my whole experience of Turkey, the impression I have gained about the Armenians, and the accounts I have heard of them on many occasions from hundreds of persons with whom I have conversed, men of the most diverse situations, sympathies, and religions, agree in regard to the general character towards which the Armenians tend, and specially as regards their faults. There is less agreement about their virtues. Some, who have merely come in superficial contact with the worst class of Armenians—rich and tyrannical, ignorant and grasping, tradesmen who have made money in narrow, sordid business in towns—deny that they have any virtues at all. But all agree that the Armenians tend towards one type, submissive to the verge of servility, accepting without attempting to resist ill treatment and insult at which a worm would rebel. Looking through the travellers that have visited Asia Minor, one sees everywhere the same account, with one single exception. Mr. Barkley, in his *Ride through Asia*

Minor, p. 87, expresses in the words of an Armenian at Sivri-Hissar, his own opinion and that of almost all the rest: "The Armenians get on well with the Turks. We are not like Bulgars and other Christians. When the Turk robs us, we see nothing; when he thrashes us, we say nothing; and so we have peace."

The author of *Anadol, the Last Home of the Faithful*, describing a journey in Asia Minor in 1852, says: "More simple and abject than the ambidextrous and vainglorious Greek, possessing sounder sense if not so much vivacity, and, above all, less imbued with national pride and ambition, the supple and self-interested Armenian humbles his brow in the dust of the lordly, pride-sowing, and poverty-reaping Moslem, and, unfeared, becomes the master of his master's all". His observations are remarkably acute, and in several respects singularly prophetic. He saw clearly the faults of the Armenian character, but was not, as so many travellers have been, blind to the promise that lay concealed beneath the surface. His experiences are well worth reading and studying; and history justifies the concluding words of his general sketch of their character: "Is not their state a subject fraught with promise, calling for inquiry, and worthy of a prying traveller's closest scrutiny?"

The sole exception to this unanimity of observation is in the pages of my friend, the " Wandering Scholar," who speaks of the Armenian's " ineffaceable nationalism, his passion for plotting and his fanatical intolerance ". He declares that "there are few Armenians who have not committed technical treason by becoming members of such societies [1] at some period of their lives ". He speaks of the " Kurd behind the Armenian, and the Russian behind the Kurd," or, again, of the Kurd as " now cutting an Armenian's throat, now leaguing with him in a war on a hostile tribe," giving his readers in the west the impression that the Kurds and Armenians are two sets of unruly and quarrelsome barbarians, at one moment bickering with one another, at another uniting in hatred of common enemies (such as the Turks, the western reader naturally infers from the whole tone of the passage, though that is not actually stated in brief, quotable assertion).

It was not easy for me to see how the " Wandering Scholar " reached a view so diametrically opposed to all I have seen or heard or read ; and yet I know that he judges here from what he saw and what he heard. In the following pages I shall try to bring out the facts, contemplation of

[1] *Viz.*, " Armenian secret societies," mentioned in the previous line.

which prompted his judgment, and to show their relation to the facts on which most people judge. He has seen one side of Armenian life which few have seen or believed to exist—the independent, warlike Armenian — and I personally am indebted to him for the knowledge of this side, without which I should not easily have reached the conception that I entertain of Armenian character; but he has, in my opinion, given far too much prominence to a certain small number of facts (correctly apprehended in themselves), and unduly minimised or wholly omitted others, in the picture that he draws in his usual vigorous and striking style. When, however, he says that there are few Armenians who have not been members of some treasonable secret society, I must confess that this statement seems to me one of the occasional slips he has allowed himself to fall into: as when on p. 40 he heard the "shooting of bolts" on the doors of the huts of Yuruk nomads (such inventions are far too civilised and elaborate for Yuruks, or even for a Turkish village), or when on p. 15 he describes how the lady of Bol spread her petticoats over a Hittite relief to hide it from our longing eyes (the lady's dress would be more correctly described as a divided skirt). If such misuse of a name occurred in one of the historical books of the New Testament, it would be pitched upon by the critics as a conclusive proof that the book in which it occurred was a late forgery ; but I am able to certify that the " Wandering Scholar " saw the scene at Bor, and describes it with the sure touch of an eye-witness and with a keen eye for the picturesque and the comic details, but with one slip in regard to dress.

I would not have directed attention to what I believe to be the incorrectness of his statement as to the Armenians and the secret societies, were it not that the judgment which I have quoted has been used in evidence, as entirely correct, against a race which is still struggling for life against enormous odds. The reason why I have made an effort to write this book at the present time is the desire to try, however feebly, to counteract the effect of the telling indictment which the " Wandering Scholar " has brought against the whole Armenian people, as a set of conspirators. I was most unwilling to protest against his words ; for what is really mere difference of opinion between two friends is liable to be misconstrued by the public into rivalry between two competing scholars. But for the truth of history, in the urgent need of a people that is being exterminated amid the indifference or even the jeers of many, I volunteer my evidence.

The secret societies, or society, which took name from the Huntchak quarter of Constantinople, caused much harm to the Armenian cause.

Such societies are out of keeping with modern ways. It is indeed probable, or even certain, that the Greek kingdom would not have been set free from the Turkish tyranny until a much later period (if at all), had it not been for the powerful secret society which prepared and organised the insurrection; but it may be doubted if the *Ethnike Hetaireia* still continues to be of any advantage to the Greek cause. It is easy for those who live at ease to condemn the Huntchagists; and it must be confessed both that their policy was entirely unwise, in the face of the overwhelming power of Russia, to which they were running counter, and that in some respects it seems to have been not merely reckless, but morally wrong. But, after all is said, my own sympathy remains entire and unbroken on the side of the suffering people, the the vast majority of whom were wholly ignorant and innocent of the plotting.

As usual, my method shall be to give some examples from actual life, as they have come before me and gradually formed my opinions.

In 1881 we stayed a night in the town of Sandykli, a considerable place and seat of a *kaimmakam*. An Armenian came to call upon us, and entreated us to visit his house; he said he was the only Christian resident in the place, and it was so rare an event to see a Christian that he was eager to receive and welcome us. He showed us all the kindness in his power, sent wine to the house which had been placed at our disposal by the *kaimmakam*, and took a good deal of trouble to help us. As a rule, such conduct is rare among Armenians ; so far as my experience goes, they are not hospitable or disposed to take trouble to help a stranger. Persons who are strongly anti-Armenian in feeling may attribute the kindness of my friend in Sandykli to the fact that the *kaim-makam* had set the example of courtesy, being greatly impressed by the account which our Albanian servant gave of us (see p. 282). But one who cannot tell by a man's face and eyes whether his hospitality is genuine or not, is not likely to make much success as a traveller. I have not, in general, any liking for being claimed as a fellow-Christian by well-to-do but ill-educated Armenian shop-keepers. It depends very much on circumstances and persons, what emotion is roused by the claim to association and community. Many a Greek peasant, poor but full of love for education, has after some acquaintance glided insensibly into the address " Adelphe " (Brother), and I have appreci-ated it as a compliment ; but my friend the " Wandering Scholar " has seen me chuck out of the room after very short talk some conceited and familiar young Greeklings of the wealthier classes.

If I felt that the Armenian of whom I speak had a common religion with me and claim of brotherhood founded thereon, it was because his heart spoke through his eyes to mine.

In 1883, at Afiom-Kara-Hissar, the Armenian correspondent of the Ottoman Bank,[1] to whom I had a letter of credit, abused his advantage to charge 5 per cent. discount on my cheque. This was, as I knew, and as a high bank official afterwards confirmed, illegal and simple extortion ; and I declined to submit. I told him I could sell my cheque better in the open market, and left him. In the street another Armenian resident came up a few minutes later, entered into conversation, and pressed us to visit him. He took us out to his country house several hours' ride from the city, entertained us handsomely, and conversed with good sense and good feeling. Hearing about my affair with the banker, he at once said that he would cash my cheque in full ; and when I pointed out that in the circumstances it was quite fair that a certain discount should be charged, especially as my cheque was on Smyrna, not on Constantinople (where his correspondents were), he declared that he wanted to send money to Constantinople and the advantage was all on his side. In this case

[1] In 1881 there was a branch of the Ottoman Bank there, which was closed as not profitable.

nothing could be better than his action and manner throughout; and he was behaving thus to an entire stranger, whom he met in the street, about whom he knew nothing, except that I had been arrested and brought to the city by *Zaptiehs* a few hours previously on a charge of having excavated gold from the tomb of an old Phrygian chief, and that I was still under police surveillance.

Incidentally, I may remark how ready many Greeks and Armenians in the inner parts of Turkey have been to accept the cheque of a person who was to them an utter stranger. I don't know whether to attribute it to simplicity and ignorance of fraud (qualities not often attributed to either race), or to compliment myself on having honesty written on my face and them on being able to read it, or simply to see in it the proof that by long wandering and many visits I had come to be very widely known. In 1890, for example, I walked into the bazaar at Nigde, an important town, near Tyana in Cappadocia, and asked a Greek money changer whether he would cash my cheque on Smyrna. He at once said he would take it, and demanded 2 per cent. discount, evidently expecting to be beaten down. As one has usually to pay 5 per cent., sometimes even 10 per cent. discount for changing money into small silver, I thought his demand was entirely reasonable. That is only one example out of many. The only people who made difficulties about taking my cheques were officials of the bank's branches.

The Kara-Hissar banker was a typical example of the narrow, sordid, tyrannical Armenian traders ; I have seen him often, was once forced unwillingly to partake of his hospitality, when I came afterwards in less suspicious circumstances, but have liked him less each time than the preceding. Once I tried to induce him to use his influence to have a very interesting early Christian inscription and relief [1] brought to Kara-Hissar for safe keeping in the Armenian church ; but the attempt was vain. It must, however, be acknowledged that his objection —that the government was suspicious of every one who had any connection with monuments—was quite true, and in the light of recent events, the disgust I felt with his cowardly attitude is proved to have been unfair. He gauged the relation in which he stood to the government better than I. The recent persecution has been directed against every sign of interest in the past, as showing a tendency to revive Armenia.

Take two more instances of this class of Armenian. In the end of May, 1883, we came to Serai-Keui,

[1] Published from a drawing by Mrs. Ramsay in my *Church in the Roman Empire*, facing p. 440, and *Cities and Bishoprics of Phrygia*, p. 736.

at the newly-constructed terminus of the Ottoman Railway.[1] A khan had just been built by an Armenian to accommodate the rapidly growing traffic; and we stayed there one night. In a khan the traveller is understood to supply his own food, and we did so; but, in addition, the Armenian *khanji* pressed on our Greek cook and Turkish servant some small quantities of sugar, etc., for their evening meal; and he insisted on saving the cook the trouble of procuring the fowl, which he was ordered to buy. The Turkish muleteer who was with us was bound (according to the usual bargain) to feed himself and three horses: our two were attended to by our Turkish servant, and paid for by us.

In the morning the *khanji* sent in a bill of portentous extent, on a long and dirty sheet of paper, in which small quantities of almost every conceivable kind of grocery, with many other things which I could not read, were charged at famine prices. A night at a first-class hotel in New York would hardly have been so expensive as that night, spent on the mud floor of the yard of the khan (our room being too filthy for habitation). I sent for the *khanji* and told him I would pay him half, and that the half was triple what I ought to pay. He began to bluster and threaten. At that time, near the beginning of my work, when the Asia Minor

<hr>

[1] See p. 131 f.

Exploration Fund had just been raised, and success was problematical, I was in no humour either to spend the Fund unprofitably, or to stand a moment's trifling with a decision which had been once pronounced : success afterwards produced easier temper, but also, I fear, greater laziness. Without a word, but merely showing half the amount of the bill ready in my hand, I ordered the horses to be prepared and loaded; when this was done, every one mounted, and we started ; I offered the money once more in vain, put it in my pocket, and rode out last of all; the *khanji* came up and laid his hand on the reins to stop me ; my riding-whip came down sharply on his hand, and he drew it back. I never saw him again ; but near three months afterwards, when I was at Serai-Keui again, a servant from the *khanji* came and asked for the money, which was paid at once. This incident caused some talk and general pleasure in Serai-Keui, where the *khanji* was cordially detested and much feared.

At Sivri-Hissar in 1883 I was greatly delighted with the beautiful glossy socks[1] of Angora wool which are sold there. One of our servants bought a pair ; and I told him to go and get twenty pairs for me, intending to send some as gifts to deserving friends at home. He came back, saying that the

[1] See p. 274.

Armenian, from whom he had bought his pair, did not possess so many, but would try to procure them. Next morning, as we were ready to start, the socks were delivered, and hastily put into my bag. On the following day, I took out a pair to put on ; and the very sight of them, glistening like silk, was cool and refreshing. Each pair was bright, and clean, and glossy white; and each was so arranged that one sock was concealed within the other. In the first pair, the inner sock was a tattered rag of common wool; and on trial every pair was the same. I had twenty good socks and twenty bad. The Armenian had procured twenty worn-out socks, washed them, and thus made ten good pairs into twenty. Then he had watched until we were on the point of departure, when his fraud would be more likely to pass unnoticed.

These are specimens of the class of Armenian, who bring the people into general hatred and contempt. I might multiply examples ; and so could every one that has ever been in the East. In fact, ordinary travellers or tourists in Asia Minor rarely meet any other class of Armenian, for education has not been spread among the Armenians in western Anatolia, where the American missionary influence has hardly been felt.[1] In Constantinople,

---

[1] The mission stations exist chiefly in the central and eastern districts : Smyrna and Manissa are, I think, the only stations in the west.

and even in Smyrna, I have no acquaintance with the resident Armenians, having found the Greeks far more sympathetic and useful in archæological work. It is that class of Armenians of whom the author of *Anadol* says : " Using his influence and ascendency over the great, he protects the poor, to fatten on the forestalled earnings of the plough, boat, waggon, or camel, which he holds in pawn. Despised on one side, hated on the other, he is enriched alike by the Pasha and the peasant ; and well he knows the weight and power of that golden lever which he wields." Almost the entire carrying trade between the Black Sea harbours, and all parts of Asia that come into trade relations with those harbours, is in the hands of Armenians ; and the poor waggoners, camel-drivers, etc., are their slaves. A vast population of the distributing and retail trade belongs to them, except in those west and south-western parts where the Greeks are all-powerful. They are not popular, and they do not deserve to be, so far as my experience goes. But to speak of that large and powerful class of Armenians as implicated in secret societies, and as engaged at any period of their lives in plots against the government, would be as ridiculous as to accuse Messrs. Glynn, Mills & Co. of taking part in a conspiracy to blow up the Bank of England with dynamite. I even doubt if the Ottoman Government is unpopular among the majority of that class of Armenians, for Turkey is the paradise of the rich unscrupulous man, who does not shrink from using the power of the purse.

Further, that is not the class of Armenians which has given rise to the recent Imperial policy of massacre. None know better than the palace officials that their most useful, nay, their indispensable instruments in misgoverning the Empire, have always been found in that class and in a corresponding class of Phanariote Greeks. It is among the poor Mohammedan peasantry that the Armenian capitalists are hated ; and the massacres do not originate from the peasants. Generally speaking, that class of Armenians has suffered from the massacres only so far as it was necessary to appeal to the greed and envy of the Mohammedan city mob in order to rouse them to the pitch of massacre.

But that class of the Armenians cannot fairly be taken, though it often is taken, as fair specimens of the Armenian race. It is not the natural growth of the Armenian qualities and religion, it is the necessary outcome of eight centuries of Turkish rule. To appreciate what Turkish rule is, we must not go to travellers in recent years, who have seen only the condition of central and western Anatolia—roughly speaking, Asia Minor west of the Euphrates—where, for a number of years, Turkish administration has been carried on under constant dread of European interference, and where the Christian population has been saved from wrong by that dread. Yet even there, take the following example out of many which reached my ears, on the authority of Mr. Barkley (*Ride through Asia Minor*, p. 109), not a man who has any prejudice in favour of Armenians (as any reader of his book will see). " In October, 1877 . . . at an Armenian village, eight hours from Yuzgat, a band of recruits arrived one evening. They . . . ordered the villagers to bring them everthing they had, money, food, etc. The people in a panic obeyed " . . . (only hiding their raki, which the soldiers rummaged till they found). " Then they made a hell of the place. Every woman, young and old, was insulted and outraged in presence of husband, fathers, and brothers. All the cattle, horses, and sheep were either stabbed or shot, and finally the village was burnt to the ground. Then the ruffians departed for Yuzgat, forcing the men of the village to accompany them as porters, the soldiers even riding on the men themselves ; some of the old and feeble soon broke down, but were forced to continue by being pricked forward with knives and bayonets. One old man actually died on the road." But the British consul, a man of vigour and knowledge of the country, at Angora investigated the facts, reported them by telegraph, and succeeded in compelling punishment. "The end of it all was, that the soldiers were caught, and, as all was proved to have occurred as stated, the *officer* in command *was degraded*,[1] while some of the men were sentenced to prison for five years." As Mr. Barkley remarks, this "was not a very severe punishment for wholesale rape, arson, robbery, and murder"—especially as we don't know how long the imprisonment lasted in fact—but it was sufficient to be a salutary and lasting lesson, for any exercise of official authority in punishment of crime produces an immense effect in Turkey. The consul at Angora related the same story to me in 1881, but I prefer to give it in Mr. Barkley's words (likewise derived from the consul) to add another witness.

We must, however, go back to an older time, if we want to appreciate what uncontrolled Turkish rule meant, alike to Armenians and to Greeks. It did not mean religious persecution; it meant unutterable contempt. The Turk did not mind what religion those dogs belonged to, and he was as far as possible from conceiving the wish to make them Mohammedans. They were dogs and pigs; and their nature was to be Christians, to be spat upon,

---

[1] The *italics* are Mr. Barkley's.

if their shadow darkened a Turk, to be outraged, to be the mats on which he wiped the mud from his feet. Conceive the inevitable result of centuries of slavery, of subjection to insult and scorn, centuries in which nothing that belonged to the Armenian, neither his property, his house, his life, his person, nor his family, was sacred or safe from violence—capricious, unprovoked violence—to resist which by violence meant death! I do not mean that every Armenian suffered so; but that every one lived in conscious danger from any chance disturbance or riot. Every one knew that any sign of spirit or courage would be almost certain to draw down immediate punishment; and that in bribery of the officials lay the only hope of redress, and the best chance of escape. They are charged, by the voice of almost every traveller, with timidity and even cowardice; but for centuries they had the choice offered them between submission and death. So long as they were perfectly submissive, they were allowed to live in comparative quiet; so long as they had money, they could purchase some immunity from, or redress for, insult. Naturally and necessarily the bravest were killed off, they that could most readily cringe and submit survived, and all efforts were directed to acquiring money, as the only means of providing safety for family and self.

This account, so far from being an exaggeration, does not convey to people accustomed to safety of the person, and unused to the brutality of which Oriental nature is capable, an idea approaching the real horror of the situation in which the Christians lived in many parts—not in all parts—of Turkey. As to European Turkey, a witness of unimpeachable authority, who under the name of "A Consul's Daughter and Wife" wrote in 1878 on *The People of Turkey*, ii., p. 121, after mentioning the custom she had seen in Macedonia of holding marriages in a cellar, says: "The custom of marrying in the most retired part of the house instead of the church, among the peasants, is, according to my information, the result of the dread they had in times of oppression of giving unnecessary publicity to their gatherings, and thus inviting the cupidity of some savage band of their oppressors. . . . This state of things was brought back during recent events. Some months ago . . . in Macedonia, the bridal procession had just returned from church, when a band of Turks fell upon the house, robbing and beating right and left until they arrived at the unfortunate bride, whom, after divesting of all her belongings, they dishonoured and left to bewail her misfortunes in never-ending misery." It is a fact familiar to every person who has even the slightest acquaintance with the condition of the parts of Armenia most exposed to Kurdish incursions, that incidents of that class have always been too common to attract notice. They were, in most cases, not even special acts of revenge aimed at a special family by enemies ; they were an ordinary thing, an amusement of the district, which could be prevented among the poor only by concealing the marriage. The only difference from the Macedonian incident is that the Armenian bride was usually carried away for several days and made the property of the Kurdish village. That was the permanent condition, from which escape could be obtained only by money or by death.

It has been asserted by persons who could readily procure evidence, if they wished to find it, before making assertions, that this state of things belongs only to the last few years, and is the punishment for the intrigues and plotting of the Armenians. But in the districts where the Kurds have been dominant, such things were the rule long ago ; they were talked about, and were the subject of consular reports and ambassadorial intervention, when I first saw Turkey and began to learn what was the condition of the country. It was in the recoil from a condition like this, under the stimulating hope of British consular interference, and through the growing knowledge of European and American freedom, that the secret societies began to become important. But the great mass of the people was too ignorant and too down-trodden to take any part in the plots.

It has certainly been a thousand times worse since the Sultan took the Kurds under his protection, and gave special honours to the most outrageous among their chiefs. In former times the Kurds were considered enemies of the government, and the officials in the feeble, helpless, incapable way in which Turkish administration is conducted, made a show of trying to protect their Armenian subjects from them. But under the present Sultan, such a pretence ceased. In the style of the pugnacious Irishman, trailing his coat through the village, and asking " if any gintleman would tread on the tail of it," your Kurd stalked through an Armenian village glaring round to see if any one would venture to look at him, or if any one would be so insulting as not to be doing what the barbarian's momentary caprice chose to consider that the wretch ought to be doing. The only way in which the miserable peasant could make sure of giving no insult to the Kurdish ruffian, as he stalked through the place, was to keep out of his sight; on those who offended him the punishment was inflicted in in-describable brutality, by people whose amusement and talk, whose jests and cursing, lie in extremes of horror, surpassing the disgustingness of those crimes which seem to us so unnatural as to imply insanity in the perpetrators.

To appreciate what was the situation to the verge of which the Armenians were often brought and which they felt as a danger continually threatening them in case they displeased their masters and a riot was roused, one must conceive what has been always the character of a thorough-going Turkish massacre. It does not mean merely that thousands are killed in a few days by the sword, the torture, or the fire. It does not mean merely that everything they possess is stolen, their houses and shops looted and often burned, every article worth a halfpenny taken, the corpses stripped. It does not mean merely that the survivers are left penniless—without food, sometimes literally stark naked. That is only the beginning, the brighter and lighter side of a massacre in Turkey. Sometimes, when the Turks have been specially merciful, they have offered their victims an escape from death by accepting Mohammedanism. But as to the darker side of Turkish massacre—personal outrage and shame—take what the more freespoken historians of former times have told ; gather together the details of the most horrible and indescribable outrages that occasional criminals of half-lunatic character commit in this country ; imagine those criminals collected in thousands, heated with the hard work of murder, inciting each other and vying with each other, encouraged by the government officials with promises of impunity and hope of plunder— imagine the result if you can, and you will have some faint idea of the massacres in the eastern parts of Turkey.

There has been no exaggeration in the worst accounts of the horrors of Armenia. A writer with the vivid imagination of Dumas and the knowledge of evil that Zola possesses could not attain, by any description, the effect that the sight of one massacre in the Kurdish part of Armenia would produce on any spectator. The Kurdish part of Armenia is the "black country". It has become a charnel house. One dare not enter it. One cannot think about it. One knows not how many maimed, mutilated, outraged Armenians are still starving there.

Further, to rightly appreciate the educative surroundings in which Turks grow up, one must remember that such massacres were preached and roused and led by the priests, who set the example in some cases of treating the murder of Armenians as a holy sacrifice, and who promised special honour in Paradise to all who joined in the holy work, teaching that massacre and outrage of Giaours is a religious merit.

But it is not the case that all Turks in any city took part in massacre. The better class disapproved; many regretted; some even tried to save Armenian friends. It must be remembered that it needs an extraordinary strength of emotion to rouse a Turk to actual interference with what he regards as the will of God; and their natural view was that the massacre had been willed by God and the Padishah, and the fact must be accepted; and yet some did interfere. But the city mob, after it was once roused by priests and officials, revelled in the work. The conduct of the blacks in the island of S. Domingo, when they rose against the planters and the garrison, and murdered almost everybody, furnishes the nearest parallel to Armenia; but there the planters retaliated.

In the course of years in an uneasy and uncertain country, it has been strongly impressed on my mind that the higher moral development is hardly possible for a class or a race, until it has obtained security for the person. The first gift of God to man is his body; that gift is man's free possession, which no other man has any right to slay or to vitiate; and safety of the person lies at the basis of moral progress. So long as men live with the possibility of murder and outrage present before their minds, the higher qualities of character cannot be developed. Even the most trustworthy, steady, and disciplined troops, and their officers,[1] tend to become demoralised by long exposure to unseen and incalculable attacks ; but when a race or clan of men spends its existence from childhood upwards in such a situation, life degenerates into a craven and degrading scramble for safety ; and if safety can be gained best by ignoble acts, then only they survive that are quick to act ignobly.

But, it may be said, the Armenians have been craven to accept this lot, and should have preferred death. Let those who have proved that they could themselves choose death in preference to a slave's life, cast reproach at them ; and those who reproach the Armenians that have lived are all the more bound to approve the Armenians that have rebelled.

The Armenian, as he is after eight centuries of slavery, has been described in the preceding pages. But there remains a small group of Armenians free and unconquered by the Turks. In the fastnesses of the Taurus mountains there exists a remnant of the once powerful Armenian kingdom, which ruled over great part of Cilicia and the adjoining hill-country of Cappadocia and Isauria for several centuries, after the rest of eastern and central Asia Minor had become a Turkish possession. It was a

---

[1] I speak not without testimony from men, whose tried courage has made their name familiar to the world.

prince of these Armenians who welcomed Barba-
rossa and his crusading army on their toilsome
march from Konia over Taurus to the southern sea,
a few days before the great German Emperor
perished prematurely in the waters of the Kaly-
kadnos. If the Armenians subject to Turkey tend
towards a timid and submissive type, the contrast
of the free Armenians proves that the timidity is
the result of the long repression and the "reign
of terror". The few thousands of free Armenians
of Zeitun maintained their freedom against all
efforts of the Turks till 1879, when the modern
cannon of a large army compelled a surrender. By
ambassadorial intervention (English mainly, I believe), the intended general massacre was prevented;
but a fort was built commanding Zeitun. Again,
in the desperation caused by the massacres of the
last few years, Zeitun rebelled, captured by assault
the fort, held, though it was, by superior numbers,
and resisted for months every attack of a Turkish
army far more numerous than all the Armenians,
men, women and children numbered together: the
army was officered by Turks. But the Powers
intervened, "in the interests of peace"; the consuls from Aleppo came and induced the Zeitunli to
lay down their weapons, to submit to disarmament,
to give up their old flint-locks and muzzle-loaders,
with which they had beaten the improved repeating

rifles of a Turkish army.   All this was done under the solemn pledge and guarantee that, if the Zeitunli surrendered their weapons and submitted to the Turks, a Christian governor would be placed in authority over them.   Not a word more has been spoken by the Powers about a Christian governor ; and I am not sure how many of those cheated Armenians still live to be governed.

The free Armenian is not unlike the Kurd in certain characteristics.[1]   The faults to which both tend are graspingness and selfishness, in contrast to the Greeks, who tend rather towards the faults of vanity and display.   Both free Armenian and Kurd cling desperately to their freedom, and in the surroundings of the Turkish Empire both were unruly, a thorn in the side of the Turkish government, a terror to traders, and almost a bar to communication.   I believe that the Kurd is just the Mohammedan Armenian, and the Armenian is the Kurd passed through centuries of Christianity.   To that extent the view taken by the "Wandering Scholar" seems to me correct ; and it relates only to an exceedingly small fraction of the Armenians of Turkey.

Yet, while it is true that, of all the races with whom I have mixed in Turkey, there is none that I have personally liked less than the Armenians,

[1] On the Kurds, see pp. 47 f, 114 f.

none among whom I have found so little interest in history, none to whom I owe so little individual gratitude for kindness shown to a traveller and a guest, none who have so often treated me as a stranger whose sole interest in their eyes was the possibility of making money off him, none whose character has seemed to me generally so bound down to the estimate of life by the standard of money alone—yet I will say for the Armenians that they have furnished the most striking examples known to me of capacity to receive and assimilate and rise quickly to the level of higher education and nobler nature, when the opportunity has been placed before them by other people. It is among the Protestants that these examples most occur ; and this brings us to the subject of the American missions in Turkey (ch. ix.).

So far as I have had any experience, the priests of the Gregorian Church seemed more ignorant and on a lower intellectual level than those of any other form of Christianity that I have come in contact with.[1] For example, at an Armenian monastery three hours east of Kaisari, we had an interview with the Armenian bishop. He had entered the monastery at the age of ten, and had never been outside of its walls during the sixty years that had elapsed since then. His conversation showed as much ignorance

[1] On this subject more is said on p. 248.

of the Gospel history, as it did of the modern world. His mind, so far as any mind remained to him, was taken up entirely with trivialities and monkish legends.   The body of St. John the Baptist, or the Forerunner, as they call him, is preserved in the monastery, which is dedicated to him.   The bishop informed us that it was recorded in the Bible that, when the Jews murdered John the Forerunner at Cæsareia Philippi, John the Evangelist took the body and carried it to Ephesus.   The rest of the story, he said, was not recorded in the Bible, but had been written by the secretary of Gregory the Illuminator, the Armenian Saint: the disciples of John brought the body from Ephesus to this monastery, and there the head had been separated from the body and carried first to Constantinople and then to Rome, where (as the bishop said) it now is.   We got our Armenian interpreter (an excellent fellow, educated at Robert College) to ask what part Herodias' daughter had played in the murder of the Forerunner by the Jews; but the bishop had never heard of that lady.

The Greeks also claim to have the body of John the Baptist.   They showed it to us at the large village which stands on the estate that once belonged to the family of Gregory Nazianzen, three hours south of Nazianzos.   It was in a large chest, which contained also the head of Gregory himself, and enough of other bones (presumably of saints and martyrs) to stock a museum. We told the bishop through our interpreter that the Greeks had showed us the body of the Forerunner ; but he briefly replied, " The Greeks are liars ".

CHAPTER IX.

THE AMERICAN MISSIONARIES AND THE ARMENIAN PROTESTANTS.

I BEGAN with a strong prejudice against the American mission-work. I had heard from several sides reports that the missionaries "lend the cloak of religion to these Armenians, who use it partly to conceal their swindling, lying, cheating, and other mean vices, partly in the hope of getting a little protection from the missionaries, and through them sometimes obtaining a measure of justice". Other reports had been different; but the latter I had regarded as due to pious prejudice in favour of converts brought into the true fold, while the former seemed to me to be the cool judgment of men of affairs. Gradually, and by slow steps, I came to reverse my opinion in the light of what I saw.

It seems to me quite true that several of the Protestants whom I saw had not been converts according to the sense in which many pious people consider that true conversion must take place—the sense, *e.g.*, in which the convert is convinced of sin by a preacher of the Salvation Army. They had adopted

Protestantism from a rational conclusion that the American missionaries stood on a higher platform of life and conduct and circumstances, and were representatives of a higher civilisation and society, than the Gregorian Church. Therein lies, in my estimation, the real strength of the American missionary movement : their policy seemed to me not to be simply directed to converting persons from a different form of Christianity to their own—a policy with which I should have small sympathy in any circumstances, and none in face of the common foe. So far as I could judge, the missionaries tried to carry out what I believe to be a higher and a wiser course. In imparting education they did not proselytise. Their converts were not made in their colleges and schools. They sought, first and foremost, to organise an improved system of education for a people already Christian, but deplorably ill-educated, and debarred by the Turkish policy for many centuries from receiving any proper education ; inasmuch as any system of education among the Armenians was necessarily inconsistent with the repression of every symptom of freedom or union or organisation among them, which constituted the Armenian policy of the Turks. The reforming policy of Sultan Mahmud, after he recognised that the empire could not be maintained simply on massacres like that of the Greeks in

Scio, or of the Janissaries in Stambol, inaugurated a new era. But the Armenians themselves were too crushed and down-trodden to take advantage of it; and, moreover, there was a great difference between the intention of the Sultan in Stambol and the actual fact in Sivas or Erzerum or Mardin or Kharput. Mahmud might order that a new spirit should reign; but he could not put the new spirit into his officials in the provinces.

The American mission stepped in to offer to the Armenians what they could not make for themselves. It was under Sultan Mahmud (who died in 1839) that they inaugurated their enterprise ; and it is literally true that it was a scheme encouraged and patronised by the Imperial Government and by the most enlightened among the Turks. Both Mahmud and his two successors were favourable to the cultivation of right relations between the Christian and the Moslem sections of their subjects, and freely granted to the missionaries all the rights and privileges they needed or wished. It was, of course, not possible to eradicate the fanaticism of the Moslem town mob by an Imperial order. The early missionaries in distant cities were often in a very precarious position. Dr. Farnsworth, the senior missionary in Kaisari, a man of singularly good knowledge of Turkey, whom you might look for on his rounds through his district alike in the deepest snows of winter and the hottest sun of summer, told me that when he first went to the city, the Pasha was so afraid that anything might happen to a man who was under the Imperial protection, that he would not allow the missionary to go about the city without a guard. The whole force of conservatism, alike among Mohammedans and Armenians, was arrayed against these pioneers.

Another important fact to observe is that the Russian and French influence was used to the utmost in high quarters against the missionaries.[1] It is true that there was no alliance and little friendship between the American and the English Governments. It is also true that the missionaries have from first to last made it the foundation of their policy to avoid all political complications, to restrict themselves absolutely to their own work of education, and to be equally friendly to all civilised and civilising influences. But the two European nations, who were most opposed to British influence in the East, never for a moment wavered in the belief that the American missions were favourable to Britain, or relaxed their opposition to the missionaries. Nor was their instinct false. There is no getting over the fact that Americans and British, when they meet in a land like Turkey,

[1] See Dr. Hamlin in *North American Review*, Sept., 1896, p. 278.

feel the tie of manners and blood and religion ; and try as they might to be neutral and non-political, the missionaries could not prevent their action from producing an effect in favour of Britain. The people of the country can rarely distinguish between the two peoples, and are hardly ever quite clear whether Amellika is a part of Londra or Londra a town of Amellika.

Moreover, the missionaries were Protestant ; and the growth of Protestant spirit and sympathies is never favourable to French or Russian policy, or at least is never reckoned by French or Russians as favourable to their influence.

It is undoubtedly true that very bad feeling and even gross abuse was often shown by Gregorian or Catholic Armenians to the Protestants ; but this feeling has been painted by some writers in somewhat exaggerated terms. They hear some facts, and state them correctly, but give the incorrect impression, that there is nothing else on the other side. It is really not fair to take some scraps of private conversation, print them, and spread the idea that they convey a complete picture of a complicated and difficult historical problem. Let me give one observation on the other side. In 1882 I wrote: " In one instance I think that we found a Protestant village,[1] but usually there are only a few

[1] I cannot say whether this impression was correct or not.

Protestants in a village, while the mass of the people belong to the Armenian Church. In Comana the two parties seemed to be on very good terms. The Armenians chaffed the Protestants for their laziness and gluttony, and declared that they had changed their religion only to avoid the frequent church-going on saints' days and the long fasts of the orthodox community; but it was done in apparent good humour. I went a walk in company with the Protestant pastor (who was an Armenian educated in one of the American schools) and the Armenian schoolmaster, who belonged to the Gregorian Church; and we seemed all three to be bosom friends, busied in the pursuit of Greek letters. Each of them was delighted to receive a dollar towards the expenses of his own school; and the Protestant gave me his blessing in quite patriarchal style when I departed." I do not give this as the whole truth. The missionaries had to contend long against the enmity of the Gregorians; but, with the Armenians' intense devotion to their down-trodden Church, it is not unnatural that many of them should have regarded the missionaries with extreme and bitter hatred. It was an unavoidable stage in a social process; but it was only a stage; and in recent years it has to a not inconsiderable extent been surmounted.

It is, then, quite true that the missionaries had

almost every influence against them except the three former Sultans, though there were occasional examples of generosity among the provincial Turks, as when one refused to sell a piece of land for the Central Asian College in Aintab, but presented it as a gift to those who were unselfishly trying to benefit his country. But, in spite of every obstacle, the mission grew into one of the greatest and most beneficent organisations that have ever been elaborated by private enterprise and skill. Robert College in Constantinople is the central point, and I think the earliest; and I believe firmly that Robert College has done more to render possible a safe solution of the "Eastern Question" in European Turkey, than all the ambassadors of all the European Powers have succeeded in doing to render that solution difficult; and the reason is that the missionary colleges have sought neither to gain anything themselves nor to prevent others from gaining anything, whereas the whole aim of the diplomacy of every European Power has been first to prevent any other from gaining anything, and secondly to achieve some selfish gain.

An educated middle class is almost entirely absent from Oriental countries and Oriental society, in which there are only a monarch and his slaves, some more favoured, some less, but all equally de-

pendent on his caprice. Free constitutional government depends on the existence and strength and
good sense of this educated middle class ; and the
larger it is in comparison with the privileged class
on the one side and the destitute class on the other,
both more or less unproductive and both more or
less drawbacks to the freedom of the state, the
better it is for the whole nation.

The work of the American missionaries has been
to produce an educated middle class in the Turkish
lands ; and they have done it with a success that
implies both good method in their work and good
raw material to work upon.   I have come in contact
with men educated at Robert College in widely
separate parts of the country, men of diverse races
and different forms of religion, Greek, Armenian
(Gregorian), and Protestant ; and have everywhere
been struck with the marvellous way in which a
certain uniform type, direct, simple, honest, and
lofty in tone, had been impressed on them.   Some
had more of it, some less ; but all had it to a certain
degree ; and it is diametrically opposite to the type
produced by growth under the ordinary conditions
of Turkish life.

Now, let me give a few specimens taken at
random among the Protestants with whom I have
come into relations.   In 1884, in a khan at Afiom-
Kara-Hissar, where we stayed a day, an Armenian

came up and entered into conversation in English. His English was not perfectly correct, nor did he speak it with ease; but it was really remarkable that he should have picked it up so well with his slender opportunities. He told me that he was a Protestant, related some part of his history (which I cannot remember), and inquired carefully about the means of getting out to America. He was a watchmaker; but, as he said, there was no trade and no possibility of getting work or earning money in Turkey. America, where the missionaries came from, was the goal of his ambition. His appearance and manner reminded me much of a decent, steady Scotch shopkeeper, rather slow, respectably educated, taking a fairly wide interest in the world, making the best of his opportunities, and with a shrewd eye to the main chance: not a lofty type of nature, but a good average man, indicating a strong and healthy stock, from which would spring many others of the same vigorous mould.

Again, in a remote village, on the site of Comana, buried in a glen of the Anti-Taurus, I met in 1890 a young Armenian pastor, on a round of inspection of the stations in his district. Meeting him accidentally and unawares in the squalid street of that mud-built village, I felt, as he approached, the air of education and refinement and high purpose which belonged to him. He had been trained first at the

College of Aintab, and afterwards at a Theological Seminary in America.   Naturally, his superior opportunities placed him on a much higher intellectual level than most of the other persons whom I refer to in this chapter.   It is incidents like that accidental meeting in a dark country, which bring home to one's mind the power that education and unselfish aims and lofty ideas exert to ennoble the mind and look of man, surrounding him as it were with a light from heaven.   And when I think that it is men of that stamp who have been the object most aimed at in the recent persecution, and have been given over to the vulgar town-mobs to batter to death with bludgeons, or to slay by torture and mutilation, I can hardly continue my round of work in my own country.   My own personal liking, and gratitude for help received, are far greater to the Turkish villagers than to the Armenians ; but a character and purpose like those of that young Armenian are so far above the Turkish level as to be inconceivable even to the best of them.

As the next example I shall take an Armenian, who was not in communion with the American missionaries, the founder and first head of a new Protestant Armenian Church.   As he was, or is (I know not if he escaped the recent massacre), a noteworthy type, I shall quote two accounts of him, written independently, and giving very different estimates of the man.   The first is taken from Mr. Barkley's interesting and instructive book,[1] in which he mentions "the native Armenian pastor, 'an honourable man,' which means, in the language of Kaisari, a man of some social standing. We were evidently expected to be greatly impressed by him . . . though I cannot say either his appearance or manners were very prepossessing. He was a short, dark man, with bushy whiskers and beard that were pushed forward in a fringe in front of his face by high though somewhat flabby stand-up collars; his dress was a parody on that of an English clergyman. . . . He told us he had visited Scotland for the purpose of collecting money for a Church, and had been very successful there. . . . He abused the Turks a little, but he abused the Catholic and other Armenians very much more. . . . Altogether his conversation did not make any lasting impression on us beyond a general conviction that, if the Turks were removed out of the way for a short time, the three denominations of Christians would cut each other's throats."

Like everything else that Mr. Barkley says about Turkey, this is a picture sketched from the life, vivid and real.   But it gives only the superficial

---

[1] *A Ride through Asia Minor*, p. 153.

impression of an evening visit. There is no explanation suggested why the pastor was "an honourable man," or why educated and polished Americans expected that he should make a "great impression" on English strangers; when one asks these questions, one sees that there must surely have been more in the native pastor than appears in the very unprepossessing picture (the most repellent parts of which I have omitted). But readers generally will treat the picture as a complete account of "an honourable man" in Kaisari. The fact that European clothes are a sad trial to the Oriental, whether Turk or Armenian, and that he never feels at home in them, is correctly appreciated and brought out in his own vivid way by Mr. Barkley. It is often worse among the Europeanised Turks. The use of buttons is hard for the Turk to learn; he looks on them as mere ornaments; and the consequences are sometimes rather startling. Even the most Oriental of Armenians who adopts European costume has made himself master of the buttons, but the relation between collar and shirt sometimes evades him; and Mr. Barkley brings out the consequences at considerable length, and with perfect accuracy. But there was much in the native pastor more worthy of note than the hiatus visible at times between his collar and his shirt. In the *Scotsman*, 4th Nov., 1882, I tried to describe what seemed to me remarkable in the man ; and I may here quote verbatim what was there printed, nine years before Mr. Barkley's book was published, 1891.

"In Kaisari of Cappadocia we found the most interesting of these Protestant communities. It was not connected with the American mission, and the pastor had belonged from his infancy to the Protestant Church. He had been educated at one of the American schools, and had afterwards come to Edinburgh, where he attended divinity classes. We lived in his house for a week [1] and found it most cool and pleasant in the heat of July. The church was built beside the house ; both were constructed with money contributed chiefly in Edinburgh, and both did great credit to the architectural skill of the workmen of Kaisari. The pastor had forgotten most of his English, but he had evidently profited by his visit to a civilised country. He has organised his little church in accordance with the Turkish law, and has thus given it a legal footing in the land. The principle of the law is that a religious body can be recognised only through its head ; the Government allows complete freedom to every religion, but requires that the Church shall have a head, through whom all communications between the Government and the Church take place. The pastor

[1] The military Vice-Consul at Kaisari had rented it from the pastor.

got his church officially recognised as the Armenian Protestant Church ; he is the head of this Church throughout the Turkish Empire. He is a member of the *Medjliss* (Local Government Council), and has the legal right to nominate a head over his own church in every district of the Empire ; the man whom he nominates has then a seat in the Government Council of his district. This stroke of policy may have important consequences in the future history of this district, as it relieves the members of this body from some difficulties that beset the American Protestants."

As to the pastor's work on the *Medjliss*, Dr. Farnsworth gave me, as characteristic of the man, an account of the way in which he made his mark, and became a person of weight in the city. The Pasha was bent on carrying through a stroke of the usual policy, much to his own benefit, but advantageous to no one else. He required that the members of the Council should sign a document, which he wanted in carrying out his policy. He explained what he desired, and made it clear that he was determined to have it ; and, of course, he had privately arranged with some of the members to set the example of signing. The document reached the pastor : he declined to sign it. They pressed him by argument, by threats of danger, by showing that no interest of his own was affected by the Pasha's policy, and by hints of advantage to be gained, if he signed. He steadily declined to put his signature to a document, which he knew to be false. The Pasha was furious, but he could not venture to carry through his policy in the face of this action, and the document was withdrawn. To us it seems a creditable thing ; but those who know how the Armenians have been brought up to cringe before a Pasha from fear of death, will find something heroic in the pastor's conduct, sacrificing his own private advantage to the interests of truth and the public welfare, and they will overlook the hiatus between his collar and his shirt, lest the saying about the hero and his valet be applied to them.

The skill and the initiative shown by the Protestant pastor at Kaisari in suiting his plans to, and taking advantage of, the law as it existed were all the more striking when one observed the situation in which the missionary congregations were placed. In this respect there is an interesting analogy between them and the position of the earliest Christians in the Roman Empire. In both cases the state law demanded that the organisation, if officially recognised, should have a distinct head both as a whole and in each separate part, through whom it might communicate with the government. In both cases it was difficult to comply with such a requirement, for there was not a distinct and single head of the organisation. The analogy cannot here be pursued in detail, as qualifications and chronological variations come in; but it is an interesting repetition of history. The Turkish Empire is the representative of the Roman Empire, the Armenian mission has many points of resemblance to the primitive Church. Moreover, the missionaries would have one serious difficulty in appointing either a supreme head, or heads of the local parts, apart from the fact that such a system is inconsistent with American congregational organisation. The Turkish law could not recognise any head (whether really so or only nominated as a representative) who was not a Turkish subject; but even if a foreign man [1] were willing to become a Turkish subject, it is impossible, being expressly forbidden by the capitulations regulating foreign relations with the Empire.

The tedious intervention of consuls and ambassadors must often be employed by the missionaries, when a constituted head might deal directly with the Imperial Government. I know from friends, who have had a large stake in Turkey, that the slowest and most uncertain way of getting anything

[1] Women could become Turkish subjects; and, at the time when foreigners could not themselves hold landed property in Turkey, they often held it in their wife's name.

from the Porte would be by setting in motion consular and ambassadorial machinery. On this subject, however, least said, soonest mended ; though
many stories might be told.

Mr. Barkley, in the work just referred to, gives
a very unfavourable account of the Armenian
Protestants ; and, undoubtedly, it cannot be denied
that members of the body could be found, whose
character and motives were no better than his
description. But my deliberate opinion is that he
applies to the whole body language which is true
only of the worst specimens ; and the conduct of
the Protestants during the recent years of massacre
emphatically and triumphantly disproves his estimate of them. The truth seems to me to be that
Mr. Barkley could not stand the welcome which
they gave him, as he arrived at Kaisari, when a
band of about sixty Protestants were on the outlook
to receive him outside the city—"old men, middle-
aged men, boys, small and great, and even quite
little children "—who all saluted him as a " Brodder".
They escorted him to the mission-house, "all
showing plainly by their scared look that they
expected to be kicked a little by every Turk they
met " ; but nothing worse befell them in the streets
than a chorus of " Giaours " and unquotable curses
of the Turkish style.

It is, certainly, not pleasant to be saluted as

"brothers" by persons unknown and unprepossessing in appearance, who slink terrified of Turks through the streets. Such familiar forms of address do not accord with English ideas and manners, and are to us, as a rule, either ridiculous or disgusting—a fact which the Socialists would be wise to recognise. But other men, other manners! Mr. Barkley perhaps was possessed of an unfortunately fraternal appearance; and hence his sad experience which evidently he could not forget or pardon. I have never been saluted as "Brodder" by any Armenian (though sometimes a Greek workman, after a certain amount of acquaintance, has slid into the address "adelphe"); but I suppose that I have not so captivating a manner and look as my predecessor in travel.

The missionaries have, perhaps, made a mistake in creating a system too rigid and inelastic. They sometimes, perhaps, aim at making their converts into American Congregationalists, which seems to me unsuitable to the Armenian character and circumstances. The true Armenian Protestantism should adapt itself more readily to the Armenian prepossessions. For example, Armenians have a prejudice that a church ought to have a dome; the pastor at Kaisari recognised this and built accordingly, and, as I think, rightly. But the missionaries hardly accommodate themselves enough to the pet conceptions of the nation.   If the Armenians think that a particular architectural form is conducive to the sacredness of a building, it is, surely, advisable to humour them.   It seems not at all necessary or wise to teach them that every one of their little prejudices is false and wrong.   But I am loath to criticise with inadequate knowledge persons whose work I admire so much as that of the American missionaries.

It is regrettable that Mr. Barkley, after enjoying the cordial hospitality of an American mission family for a week, should think it right to print such an estimate of their ways as he does on p. 152. " The missionaries in their zeal for their work even lay aside self-respect, and I think I am justified in saying so, for a man such as our host,[1] must have lost much of his before he could patiently submit to seeing his pretty, refined young wife subjected to such indignities."   It is unjustifiable to live in a man's house and then speak of him like this.   The host had a different conception of duty from his guest; but the guest seems wholly blind to the fact that it was a thousand times harder for the missionary to submit to the insult offered to his wife than to turn his own cheek to the smiter. He chose his cross, and bore it; but, though neither

[1] The name, Mr. S., is given in full.

Mr. Barkley nor I could choose it, yet I can in a sense admire the patience which I could not show, and he should refrain from joining with those Armenians whom he reprobates in insulting his host.

CHAPTER X.

THE GREEKS IN ASIATIC TURKEY.

IT would be vain and self-contradictory to try to describe the general type and national characteristics of the Greeks in Turkey. Those who are called Greeks are a religion, not a nation. They have nothing in common except the creed and ceremonial of the Orthodox Church. They have not the tie of common blood, but are the direct descendants of the most diverse races, Cappadocians, Pisidians, Isaurians, Pamphylians, men of Pontus, and so on. Their outward look and their superficial character (for I do not pretend to have seen more deeply) are often markedly divergent. They are divided by difference of language : some use Greek alone, some Turkish alone, many are bilingual. One sees Greek Orthodox churches in the eastern part of Turkey, over whose door is an inscription in Greek letters ; but when you read the words inscribed you find that they are Turkish, and on inquiry you learn that not a soul in the congregation knows any Greek except the priest. It is a remarkable fact that the Orthodox Church should have been able to bind so well together elements so diverse, and now for centuries so far divided from one another by the estranging sea of Mohammedanism, in which their scattered communities are like islets.

Perhaps, however, it is the distance between them that prevents the racial differences from being felt by the various sections of the Òrthodox Church. The lines of tribal difference of old were very clearly and strongly felt by all Greeks; and Ionians never loved Dorians, though they might unite in presence of the Barbarian. Not even the levelling and unifying effect of the Church could produce fraternal feeling between different races that acknowledged the one true Church; and, if they were close together, perhaps even now we should observe the old dislike, a trace of which we see in the occasional expressions of contempt for Galatians in the writings of the Cappadocian Saint Basil. A friend told me of a Greek village in Macedonia, where there were some outsiders from the north, not enough to have a church of their own : these attended the rites of the Greek church, and the congregation in its two sections was addressed by the priest as "Christian Brethren,—and ye Wallachians".

Hamilton mentions "that both in Trebizond and the neighbouring mountains are many Greek Turks or Turkish Greeks, a race of people who are in reality Christians, and observe the Greek rites in secret ; but who from prudential motives, profess the state religion of Mohammedanism, submit to be circumcised, attend the mosques, and practise all the other ceremonies enjoined by the Mohammedan religion " (i., p. 240). Sir Charles Wilson, who knows Asia Minor and Armenia better than almost any other living man, does not mention this class of secret Christians : they have now ceased to be under the necessity of practising this sham Mohammedanism, since a degree of toleration was encouraged by the policy of Mahmud, Abd-ul-Medjid, and Abd-ul-Aziz, and the European consuls were a great protection to the Christians until within the last few years. The nearest approach that I have observed to this pretended Mohammedanism was among Albanians. In 1891, I had an Albanian servant, who, as I learned after I had engaged him, was a Christian. Had I known in time, I should not have taken him ; but his Christianity sat as light on him as Mohammedanism does on Albanians of the northern districts ; he never acknowledged, even to my wife and me, that he was a Christian ; and he occasionally attended service in the village mosques. The Mohammedans, however, were very suspicious of him, which he explained to my wife by the fact that he wore black clothes. In other cases, too, I have noticed the utter indifference that Albanians have to Mohammedan ceremonial. In October, 1891, an Albanian servant of ours, feeling annoyed by a ragged and dirty Turk who had begun to say his prayers in the Oda, interrupted his devotions by giving him a blow with the butt-end of a gun, and then kicked him out and in derision threw after him the little carpet on which he had been praying. I was so interested in observing how far the Albanian would go that I did not interfere, as I usually did, to prevent any quarrelling between my men and the natives.

The Cappadocian Greeks are an interesting people, who have been described by the older German traveller Mordtmann (father of the present active and able physician-archæologist of Constantinople) and by the Greek Karolides, in papers that are unfortunately buried in periodicals inaccessible to most people. Cappadocia passed with hardly a struggle into the hands of the Seljuk Turks immediately after 1070, and hence it suffered little from war. The Greeks of the cities, such as Kaisari, Nigde, or Bor, forgot their Greek, until the revivification of the western spirit in the last generation produced a revival of the language. But the Greeks of the villages have retained their native language to the present day ; and it is an interesting tongue, very difficult to understand for one who, like me, had been trained in the Greek of the Ægean lands. Monsieur Karolides has published a work on this Greek dialect.

The people seemed to share in the rather suspicious temperament of the Armenian villagers, so far as my scanty experience goes. It was not so easy to get into pleasant relations with them as with the western Greeks, which was doubtless due partly to the fact that I could not catch what they said, for whereas they understood my Greek with perfect ease, their pronunciation concealed from me what they said in reply. But temperament, separation from the rest of the Greek world, and burial among the surrounding mass of Turks, had much to do with their want of cordiality to strangers, and their obvious dread of any person new to them.

The Greek Cappadocian villages are usually large and well-built, and have an appearance of comfort and wealth that contrasts remarkably with the poverty and wretchedness of the Mohammedan villages. Almost all the energy and progress visible in these regions lie among the Christians. Many of the villages make much use of rock-cutting in their domestic arrangements. At Hassa-Keui (the old bishopric of Sasima to which Basil consecrated the reluctant Gregory), Melegob (Malakopaia), etc., every house has an underground story cut out of the soft rock that underlies the soil of the level fertile plain. Narrow passages connect the underground chambers belonging to each house, and longer but equally narrow passages run from house to house. A big solid disc of stone stands in a niche, outside each underground house, ready to be drawn forward in front of the door at any alarm.

Other villages use the rocks of the hillsides, of which Gelvere (the old Karbala, the estate inherited by Gregory of Nazianzos) may serve as one out of many specimens. It is situated in a narrow rocky glen, which is from end to end a mass of rock-cut chambers, cells, churches and houses. The prospect down the glen from the upper end is marvellously quaint and fantastic: the soft rocks have been worn into odd shapes by the weather: the rock cuttings add to the curious appearance: the modern houses, well built of cut blocks of the same stone, can hardly be distinguished from the actual hillside.

The people of these districts of Cappadocia are described as Troglodytes by Byzantine historians: and the custom of dwelling in the rocks or below the ground undoubtedly goes back to time immemorial; but we could not find any cuttings that were demonstrably pre-Christian.

At one village the water was got from wells,

which we ascertained to be about 300 feet deep. A cumbrous, rude, quaint contrivance was used, whereby the united strength of four women drew up a tiny bucket. I timed them, and found that about forty-five seconds were required for the ascent of a bucket.

At one of these villages we were mistaken for the Bishop of Kaisari, who was expected on a pastoral visitation. It happened that we came by the same road and reached the village about the time that the bishop was expected. Most of the population was gathered to welcome him ; and the priests with a choir of boys headed the procession that was coming forth to meet him and welcome him. Suddenly we rounded a rocky corner of the narrow road, and came within view of the pious band about forty yards distant. Strangers are rare in this corner of Cappadocia ; and the eager villagers at once concluded that we were the bishop's party. The choir struck up a hymn, the priests made various motions with their hands, and everybody raised his voice in welcome. The situation was embarrassing to our humility ; and the explanation was not easy to make without embarrassing the villagers. Fortunately we saw a curious monument in a rock to the left of the road, so we went off to examine it, making as if we observed nothing. The shouting ceased, the priests stood motionless, the choir stopped voice by voice. I never learned what they thought of us, nor whether they recovered their voices in time to welcome the bishop.

The contrast between the condition of the clergy in the Armenian and in the Greek Church may be illustrated by the two bishops of the region round Kaisari. The Armenian bishop has been briefly described on p. 217. In our interview with the Greek bishop, German was the medium of communication, for the bishop spoke that language with ease. He was a man of information, wide experience, and great business capacity, and had been one of the representatives of the Greek Church at the conference, which was held, if I rightly remember, in Bonn, to discuss the scheme of union between the English and Greek Churches, favoured by Canon Liddon and some other members of the English Church. As we were talking with the bishop I pictured to myself how the man of Kaisari would be sure to accept with grace and real pleasure every concession made by the English representatives, but when any concession was asked on his side, would politely and suavely explain that it was impossible for the " Orthodox Church " to swerve a hair's breadth from the Orthodox Faith. He made on me the impression that the Orthodox Faith was to him a matter more of enthusiastic pride than of real religious conviction; but I may be wronging him, for one cannot gauge a man's whole character in an hour's conversation. Undoubtedly his interest lay in the direction of affairs and the modern world of politics, not in that of ancient history or the Church Fathers (towards which all the talk had been directed, when in 1880 I was conversing in Greek, not German, with the Bishop of Aidin in the Mæander valley). We did not tell the Bishop of Kaisari how we had been mistaken for him, which was an unfortunate omission. I should like to know how he would have taken it.

It is probable that the two bishops of Kaisari are extreme representatives in opposite directions of their respective Churches. Some of my friends have taken exception to my statement in the *Contemporary Review*, September, 1896, p. 446, about the extremely debased condition of the Armenian Church; but it seems not unfair to write rather strongly, when such a marked contrast between the two corresponding dignitaries at such an important city as Kaisari came before one's notice; for in the episcopal system, such bishops imply much about their Churches. In the Byzantine hierarchy, the Bishop of Kaisari (Exarch of the Pontic Diœcesis) always ranked first after the Patriarch of Constantinople.

A contrast is frequently drawn between the grasp-ing nature of the Greek and the generosity of the Turk. So far as my experience goes this con-trast is often much exaggerated. I have had more difficulties in bargaining with Turks, especially when I was new to their ways, than I ever had with Greeks, and found them in a small way quite as grasping as any Greeks are. The same persons who will entertain the traveller very hospitably, following the hereditary custom without thought and without deliberate choice, will often try as hard as the most grasping Greek or Armenian to extort an exorbitant price from him, if it comes to be any question of a bargain. In such cases there is this great difference between the Greek and the Turk or Turkmen : the former has some con-ception of the comparative value of things, and is therefore easier to deal with on a uniform scale, but the latter is often ignorant of the relative value of money and commodities, and may sell his eggs and milk absurdly dear or ridiculously cheap. It is therefore too difficult for the archæological tra-veller to carry out his own ideas of right and fair pay-ment. Very often his resolve to pay for everything may lead only to dispute and almost to quarrelling ; and in 1881 my attempt to deal with the villagers on the principle of fair trade made that journey a scene of frequent bickering. In one case my servant was asked a sum equivalent to six shillings and eightpence for a dish of kaimak (thick clotted cream); and when he appealed to me against this imposition there was a tremendous scene of clamour and complaint. I have known a whole Turkmen camp (and Turkmens as a rule are exceedingly hospitable) refuse to sell a pot of milk lower than about six times the price of milk in London ; and yet flocks by the thousand were round the camp. As a whole my experience is that you will save much trouble, and will leave the village much better pleased, if you avoid rousing their expectations of payment ; try as far as possible to arrive with few wants (bringing with you some articles from a previous camp), claim these as a matter of hospitality (rewarding the givers by *bakshish*, not by formal payment), and purchase at the last some things for the next camp. The instinct to trade and to haggle and to extort is just as real in the Turk as in the Greek ; but in the former it is often dormant, owing quite as much to pure ignorance as to real generosity. I have experienced, proportionately, at least as much kindness and generosity and hospitality among Greek villagers as among Turks ; but, as it happens, I have stayed at a hundred times as many Turkish villages as at Greek.

Among the richer Greeks the archæologist, if he shows any affability and Hellenism, will always find the most cordial welcome, lavish hospitality, and zealous co-operation in all his schemes of exploration. No words can be too strong to describe their kindness to me. Naturally, if one is stuck-up and standoffish in his manner, he is not so welcome. My lot, however, has lain so much more among the Turks, that I have not often come into relations with Greeks since 1881.

While there is singularly little diversity of opinion about the Armenians, there exists extraordinary contradiction between the opinions entertained about the Greeks by competent observers of long experience. To take two examples out of many, I may give the testimony of two persons, British by nationality, both possessing long and intimate acquaintance with business in Turkey, and deserving as well as holding a leading position in it. One of them, Scottish by birth and training, could hardly contain himself if the name of Greek was mentioned in his hearing, and could not restrain himself from abusing the whole people as knaves and cheats: on the other hand he was in the closest business relations with Armenians, and I never heard him say a word against them as a class. The other person, born and trained in the country, and controlling a business that brought him into relations with many Greek firms in various parts of the country, declared to me often that he had never found the slightest difficulty in dealing with his Greek correspondents, that he had not been cheated nor deceived by them, that he never found it necessary to enter into formal written contracts with them as was the practice with English firms, but a word spoken on each side was accepted and loyally carried out by both.

The opinion of a stranger about the Greeks of western Asia Minor would be strongly affected according as he came in contact with one or the other of these two excellent authorities. Which are we to believe?

For my own part, I think the second is nearer the truth, provided you remember that much depends on the tone and spirit in which you deal with the Greeks. In the East, business has rapidly changed from the native system, in which every small bargain was a contest of skill between two single adversaries, each of whom tried to out-manœuvre the other, to the European system. The morality of business in England is said not to be so very high, at least in some departments; and it is believed that one cannot safely accept every representation, made even by responsible and respectable boards of directors, as to the state of the enterprises in which they ask the public to invest money. Naturally, the traders of the East are influenced a great deal by the general tone of the firms with which they are brought in contact : expect them to act as cheats, show them clearly that you expect it, and you are not likely to be disappointed.

But there is another side to the case, and, though I went out well primed with advice to distrust the Greeks, to be always on my guard against being cheated, to regard every one as a knave, I found it unprofitable and unnecessary as time went on to dread such bad treatment, and easier, as well as safer, to deal with them in a different spirit. Of course, you must keep your wits about you and your eyes open ; you will find consummate scoundrels among the Greeks (just as you may, without the help of Democritus's candle, find them among the Scotch or the English), and you must in all three nations discriminate and select. But it is, of course, harder to discriminate between men of a strange race, and the foreigner is liable to fall into mistakes on this score which the native would avoid. But it is as unfair to condemn all Greeks, because you may be cheated in your first business arrangement, as it would be to say that Jabez Balfour is a typical and fair specimen of all British company promoters.

I take one example of the necessity of understanding the men with whom you have to deal in your wanderings. The few Greeks whom you meet in the purely Turkish country, where most of my time was spent, are tradesmen or emissaries sent out by Smyrniote dealers in antiquities. These do not know the comparative value of coins, but they are well aware that some coins are worthless, others valuable, and a few invaluable; and, in general, when they show you a number of coins their object merely is to find out which are the valuable ones. If you make an offer for one or two, they infer that these are good; but they won't sell, for they are certain that you are offering only a quarter or a tenth of the real value, with the view of making a big profit in Smyrna or in Europe. If you offered them £10 or £50 for a bronze coin, they would conclude that it was one of the great rarities, and would resolve to demand £100 or £200 in Smyrna.

This is a peculiarly aggravating way of dealing, as well as bad business; and you are apt to feel angry and sore, as I have been more than once, when a price far beyond the market value in London was refused for a coin so worn that I could not decipher it, which I wished to have because it might prove decipherable with time and then afford evidence regarding the name of the site where it had been discovered. Then one feels inclined to echo the dictum of a distinguished English archæ-ologist, who lived long in the Ægean lands, that a

Greek who had sold you a coin for four times its value would be ready to hang himself with chagrin if he found reason to think that he might have got five times the value by a change of tactics.   But you must take men as you find them, and not be angry because they are ignorant and suspicious.   Their suspicion springs to a great degree from their ignorance; and I think it is the same to some extent with the English suspicion of Greeks. They feel that they don't know the Greeks well enough to estimate individual character, and distrust all alike.

After I found out their ways, I never named a price to these Greek emissaries; for, when they have gained their object in discovering which are the more valuable coins, they often conceal them forthwith, and won't permit you a second glance. If there is any coin of interest, of which you wish to make a note, you will be wise not to sort it out, but to keep it along with the rest, and go on talking in a general way; meanwhile you can identify it, and fix its description in your memory; but as soon as you begin to write down a description they snatch the whole set away from you, for they suspect that the value of the good coin will be diminished, if it gets into your book.   My friend, the " Wandering Scholar," is troubled in conscience at having once taken part in this method of acquiring knowledge[1] against the will of the owner; those who have any doubt as to the morality of the act would be wise not to engage in it; but my view is clear that the crime is with him who allows knowledge to be hid.

As might be expected the Greeks of the Ægean coast-lands approximate more in character to the Greeks of Greece; but they resemble not so much the idle crowd that throngs every café in Athens all day long, as the vigorous-looking members who represent the country districts in the Boulé. Whether the resemblance holds true in regard to those qualities which have always prevented the Greeks from forming a strong nation and a strong government, it would be hard to say. In Athens, certainly, one feels that the modern Greeks, like the ancient, have not yet learned to obey laws, and therefore cannot make them. They are better and more prosperous under almost any other government than they are under their own. The old jealousy and distrust which each district entertained of its neighbours still reigns; and each district seems to devote more attention to preventing its neighbours from getting an undue share of attention and advantage than to forwarding its own interests; while all join in opposing the foreigner, and in

[1] See p. 13 of his entertaining book.

preventing him from gaining anything out of them. Thus Greece has not developed as it might have done under a firm rule, which enforced obedience to a well-considered plan for the general advantage. It has not been too fortunate in its kings, for nothing good could come from Otho, whom the Powers seem to have selected in a rough practical joke, on the principle that anybody was good enough for so small a kingdom as Greece ; while the present king, though well-intentioned, has not the firmness and vigour that would be needed to make a mark in any department of life.

What has been said about Turks and Greeks points to the conclusion that a union of their qualities is needed to make a strong and self-sufficing nation. Each seems to possess some good qualities which are lacking in the other. Take the best among each race, and compare them. The Greek can be brave, but you can never trust him to die at his post or to fight to the bitter end in the face of discouragement and despair. The Turk will maintain his trust till he is cut in pieces, and will stand at his post till he falls ; but he is devoid of resource and ingenuity, and is hardly ever able to command or to organise the strength of a number of other men, which the Greek can do. In every department of practical life, you want to have men of both races on your staff; and it has always seemed to me that " the Turks and the Greeks will united make a happier country than either race could by itself". So I wrote in 1890, and so I still think.

Take the two great wants in the life of the Turks, as they have been repeatedly brought out in these pages. They receive no rational or systematic training, whether moral or intellectual; but the strongest quality of the Greeks, and their greatest achievement in the world, greater even than their art, their poetry, or their science, has been their love for education and their careful provision for it in their cities.[1] The Turkish women grow up in such circumstances as to dwarf their intellectual faculties and to enfeeble or pervert their moral qualities, so that they are quite unfit to communicate any proper bent and training to their children's minds. The ancient population of Asia Minor, on the contrary, gave an unusually high position and influence to women;[2] and it is Mohammedanism that has destroyed the old respect shown to them; but among the Greeks, as I have said, p. 49, the women of the peasant classes seemed to me better than the men.

In union and amalgamation of the races, then

[1] *Cities and Bishoprics of Phrygia*, i., p. 440.
[2] *Church in the Roman Empire*, pp. 67, 403.

lies the hope of Asia Minor, and to that end all
the efforts of a wise government should be directed.
The country seems to me to be full of hope and
the promise of life and growth, and to contain all
the elements required for a vigorous and happy
race. The bar of religion stands in the way of
amalgamation ; but the example of the third century shows that the bar is not indestructible. I
have pointed out elsewhere [1] how, under a government that simply enforced quiet and order, the
two diametrically opposed religions, Christianity
and Paganism, flourished peacefully side by side,
and regulated their own mutual relations without
difficulty. Similar is the case at the present day,
wherever a vigorous governor or consul maintains
order and quiet, and holds the balance even.
That easy prosperous development in the third
century was ruined by the policy of massacre in
the period 303-312 A.D.; and, after beginning in
recent time, it is again being destroyed by the
same means.

Postscript.

Mr. Curzon is reported to have stated in the
House of Commons on 7th May, that if the Turkish

[1] *Cities and Bishoprics of Phrygia*, chapter xii.

troops were withdrawn from Candia, the result would be a massacre compared with which those in Armenia would sink into insignificance. Either the prophecy proves marvellous and utter ignorance of the character of those elements in the " Eastern Question " which Mr. Curzon is, to some degree, charged with the duty of conciliating towards one another and pacifying, or it shows a magnificent capacity for mis-stating facts so as to bamboozle and hoodwink a public which looks to him for information. The statement is one which it would be difficult to characterise in language that would not be as brutal as the offending words. But it would be disgraceful to let the statement pass without challenge, and a protest ought to be made in favour of a nation which, with many faults, has never in its worst stage been given to mutilation and orgies of personal outrage. When one must be killed, one longs for a clean death and an un-insulted corpse ; and, if either he or I have to face massacre, we shall do well to pray that we fall into the hands of Greek, not Turkish, rioters. It is probable that Mr. Curzon's words, though reported as his own, may be founded on the report of some hysterical official at the scene of action. If that be so, one begins to understand why the Cretans have never been persuaded that Britain means well by them, or is acting straight in the present business ;

and one hopes that the official may soon be entitled to honourable retirement, or that some lucrative post may be created for him in Alaska or Tierra del Fuego.

CHAPTER XI.

IN an interesting paper on "Turkish Guilds" in
the *Fortnightly Review*, December, 1896, Miss Con-
stance Sutcliffe comes forward to say a good word
for the Turks. Two institutions she mentions as
characteristic and interesting, the Janissaries and
the Trade Guilds in Constantinople. As she says,
on the Janissaries depended the *morale* of the whole
native army; but it must be kept in mind that
the Janissaries in their original conception were a
corps of Christian children, taken young from their
parents, and trained up as Moslem warriors. It
was the Janissaries who furnished the Osmanli
Sultans with a standing army, trained and educated
from infancy for purposes of war, at a time when
no other state possessed a standing army of disciplined soldiers. But though this institution shows
the wit of its founder, it constitutes no proof of the
excellence of the Turkish race.

Again, the Trade Guilds are a most interesting institution, but they were not originated by the Turks.

They are merely one of the old social facts which the Turks did not succeed in destroying. It seems to me not to admit of doubt that these same Guilds can be traced under the Roman Empire in a Romanised form, and that their origin goes back to time immemorial. They are an Anatolian institution, which has lasted under every form of government. All over the country we find proof of the existence under the Roman Empire of such Guilds as that of the dyers, or the purple-dyers, or the bakers, or the weavers of garments (these were woven in a suitable shape, so that cutting and tailoring was not nearly so much required as in modern times), with a host of others. In several cases it is obvious that the Guilds are of such fundamental importance in the classification of citizens and in the city organisation, that they must be a primeval Anatolian institution, which gave tone and direction to the growth of the Greek or Roman city.

The reader will not desire here a statement of the archæological evidence (which those who wish may find set forth at some length in the *Cities and Bishoprics of Phrygia*, i., pp. 105 ff., 440, 471); but there is not likely to be any disagreement among educated observers that the modern Trade Guilds are a mere broken-down and shadowy remnant of the old pre-Turkish Guilds, possessing far less importance in the life of the nation than they formerly did, because they are no longer so skilfully organised.

In the investigation of the social conditions that underlie the "Eastern Question," this subject is one of peculiar interest and importance. The action of the Turks in every department of life has simply been to ruin, never to rebuild. It is not merely the cities, the buildings, and the government of old Rome that they destroyed. Their work was far more thorough and far more dangerous. They destroyed the intellectual and moral institutions of a nation ; they broke up and dissolved almost the entire social fabric ; they annihilated every educative and humanising influence in the land ; and they brought back great part of the country to the primitive simplicity of nomadic life.[1] There was left just enough of the ancient institutions to make an Empire possible. Had the nomadisation of Asia Minor been absolutely complete, the nation would have been reduced to a mere set of wandering tribes ; and out of mere nomad tribes no articulated Empire can be built. It is literally true that the Turkish Empire stands on a pre-Turkish foundation, and is built up of scraps and fragments of the ruined Roman institutions. Just as the Turkish villager lives in a

<hr>

[1] See p. 103.

house built by a Christian mason, if he has anything better than a hut, and drinks water brought
in an aqueduct made by a Christian artisan ;[1] just
as the executive of Turkish administration could
not be kept up without[2] a staff of Christian sub-
ordinates to do such parts of the work as demand
a little education ; so, in general, there is hardly a
social institution in Asia Minor showing any degree
of legal or social constructiveness that is not an
older Anatolian creation, Moslemised in outward
form, and usually degraded in the process.

Even such simple associations for purposes of
social enjoyment and hospitality as that of " the
Brotherhoods," described by the Arab of Tangier,
Ibn Batuta, as characteristic of the Turkish cities[3]
of Asia Minor in the fourteenth century, seem to
have been the survival of original Anatolian institutions maintained in connection with the great
religious centres of earlier times, and preserved
under a Christianised form in the Byzantine period.
On this subject also I cannot here do more than
refer to the same work as before, pp. 96 ff., 359 f.,
630.

The permanent association of religious awe with
certain places (usually marked by natural pheno-

---

[1] See p. 22.   [2] See p. 166.

[3] He calls them " Turkmen," not " Turkish "; an interesting
point, see p. 101.

mena, indicating the presence of divine power) is an interesting subject, which shows what an intimate connection exists between the modern Mohammedans and the ancient population. The belief in the divine presence was marked in earlier time by reliefs on the rock or other works of art, by a Greek temple or by a Christian church. At the present time it is indicated, sometimes by a tree hung with pieces of rag, fastened on it by the superstition of modern devotees, sometimes by a *turbe*, a sacred building which usually takes the form of a small round edifice with a roof sloping up to a central apex, surmounted by the crescent, though various other forms occur, degenerating into the meanest type. The contrast between the stately ancient monument and the modern rag-hung tree or common-place *turbe* is typical of the degeneration of Asia Minor under the Turks. In or underneath the *turbe* is a grave, in which a *Dede* or heroised ancestor is buried or supposed to be buried. Thus the religious awe of the locality is connected with Mohammedan history or tribal heredity ; but it is older by thousands of years than the advent of Mohammedanism or of the tribe in the country. So one finds in many parts of the country places marked by the power or the grave, sometimes of persons unknown to fame (or at least unknown to me), such as Karaja Ahmed, Omar

Baba, Hadji Omar, or well-known historical personages, such as Hadji Bektash (a dervish from Khorasan, who named and blessed the first Janissaries, led them at the assault of Mudania, I think, and became their patron saint), or Seidi Ghazi (Seid the Conqueror, who led the Saracen army that was defeated at Akroenos [1] in A.D. 740). Generally there is a belief that supernatural powers of some kind or other are connected with these *turbes*, *e.g.*, that miraculous cures are effected in them.

In other cases there is no visible sign of Mohammedan belief, and yet the belief exists and is powerful. Any Ayasma or holy spring to which the Christians resort is also respected by the Mohammedans, *e.g.*, the spring of Hercules Restitutor east of Apollonia, to which the Greeks of Olu-Borlu go on an annual festival. The feast of St. Makrina at Hassa-Keui (Sasima) in Cappadocia, attracts not merely Christians but also Turks, who bring their sick animals to be cured. In the Seljuk country, certain springs are called after Iflatun (Plato), a name that originated in the time before Arab civilisation and study had completely died out of the Mohammedan world.

A quaint and enigmatical remnant, descending perhaps direct from pre-Christian times, is the

---

[1] See p. 73.

Takhtaji (woodmen), whose scanty tribes are found in widely scattered parts of the country, always in remote hill-regions, difficult of access. It is hard to gain trustworthy information about them, and impossible to learn anything of their inner life and beliefs. Outwardly they pose as Moslem, especially when they are obliged to come down to Mohammedan villages for any purpose; but it is commonly said that they are ready to drink wine and eat pork, have no mosques, and do not perform the five daily prayers. They are said to hold secret meetings, and the same scandals with regard to " Oedipodean unions " and horrid orgies are reported about them as about the early Christians. One authority, a Levantine of a well-known and much respected family, assured me on his own knowledge that they held meetings in their cemeteries; whereas others say that they meet in a house. With regard to the latter form of the current tale, Dr. Von Luschan pertinently observes that there is never any building accessible to Takhtaji which gives space for the occurrences that are related; and he explains the whole as mere lying exaggeration of Turks, who are naturally revolted both by their bad Mohammedanism and by the customs of their women, who never veil and eat along with the men.

The general opinion (to which almost all modern

observers, like the late Dr. C. Humann, Sir C. Wilson, Dr. Von Luschan, etc., incline) is that they have preserved a pre-Christian form of pagan society and rites; and that they are similar in this respect to the Yezidi, Ansarieh, and other widely scattered remnants of submerged peoples and beliefs. Their extreme secrecy makes it impossible to affirm anything about them positively; but Von Luschan [1] vouches that in two cases he has positive evidence of marriage, according to the old pagan custom, between brother and sister among them (which is one of the enormities related about them by the Turks). They live in tents or in very small, poor huts, and make a livelihood by cutting wood (whence their name).

A new form of religion is the one gift of the Turks to Asia Minor. I am by no means blind to the good qualities that exist in Mohammedanism. For tribes in a certain primitive stage of development, it furnishes a more rapid and efficacious means of improvement than, perhaps, any other religion. But it carries them only to a certain stage, and leaves them there inexorably fixed. Mohammedanism was a reinvigoration of certain Judaic and certain Christian ideas, adapted to a people still for the most part in the nomadic stage; and it is bound fast within the rigid limitations

[1] *Reisen in Lykien*, etc., Petersen and Von Luschan, ii., p. 199.

of its original social environment.   When a nation of higher social development adopts Mohammedanism, as the mass of the population of Asia Minor did when it absorbed the Turkish (as distinguished from the Turkmen) invaders into itself, the process is a distinct and fatal retrogression.   A nation cannot step backwards except in the direction of intellectual degeneracy ; and, in social organisation, the peoples of Asia Minor stepped backwards, when they became Mohammedan.

The inherent weakness and evil of Mohammedanism lies in its want of any provision for educating the young in the paths of citizenship. But how could a religion that was adapted to a nomadic people, initiate any progress or create any machinery tending towards a more developed and better articulated form of society?   In Turkey one begins consciously to realise how much of European life and thoughts and ways springs out of the educative influences which Christianity places round the child from infancy, and which parents, however much opposed to Christianity they may be, can hardly avoid.   A witness who has enjoyed the best opportunities of observing and used them well, who writes under the name of " A Consul's Daughter and Wife," but does not thereby conceal her identity from any that know Turkey, has described the effect produced on the Turkish women

by the want of educative surroundings, or rather by
the atmosphere round them of filthy joke and talk
which constitute a continuous education towards
evil, and a continuous deteriorating influence on
character. A similar feature of village life has
been alluded to above, p. 41 ff., in reference to the
young men.

Further, I am not blind to the evil character of
Byzantine rule, and have done what I can to trace
the history of its benumbing influence on the population of Asia Minor. It was the moral weakness,
the decay of education, and the growing rigidity
and want of adaptability of social institutions that
exposed the country defenceless to the Turks.
Any single city, like Philadelphia for example,
which was cut off from the enervating influence of
Byzantine administration and left free to develop
its own inherent strength and moral power in the
face of the enemy, could maintain for more than a
century its freedom and its institutions in the surrounding sea of hostile Mohammedanism, until it
was reduced to surrender to the combined armies
of a Byzantine Emperor and a Turkish Sultan.[1]
Similar was the history of the small Armenian state
of Zeitun, with its few thousands of a people, which
was a free unconquered country down till almost
yesterday. It has almost always been by the

---

[1] John Palæologus II. and Murad (Amurath), 1379.

strength or the skill of Christian allies that the Turks have vanquished the Christians;

> But Turkish force and Latin fraud
> Would break their shield, however broad.

And so it continues to be at the present day, when German intellect is pointing the way to Turkish victory over Greece.

It is perhaps the case, as some maintain, that the introduction of the Angora goat, with its beautiful silky fleece, into the country is due to the nomads; and, indubitably, the breeding and keeping of these goats is to a considerable extent in their hands. But it might be as reasonable to maintain that the nomads brought the sheep into the land, on the ground that they now have in their hands most of the flocks. I should be disposed to demand some better evidence, before accepting it as a fact that the Angora goat was unknown to the ancient inhabitants of the plateau. To take a parallel case, it is certain that the glossy black wool of the Laodicean sheep, and the violet-dark wool of the sheep of Colossae, which are celebrated under the Roman Empire and earlier, are no longer produced. Pococke in the first half of the eighteenth century saw a great many black sheep; Chandler saw only a few black and glossy in the early part of the present century; my experience agrees with Chandler's, except that I was not struck with the gloss of the few black fleeces. It is obvious that through carelessness the two breeds have been allowed to degenerate and disappear. The peculiar character of the fleeces was probably maintained by some kind of cross-breeding, and not, as some people have suggested, by any peculiar property of the water or the grass. Similarly, in the case of the Angora wool, a careful observer who had had long experience in the trade, an Englishman, whom I met at Angora in 1886, assured me that the true secret of the peculiar character of the fleece lay in the breeding. He declared as a fact known to him that the beautiful silky goats had to be crossed regularly both with the common black and the red goats (twice with the one kind, once with the other) in a certain number of generations: I cannot trust myself to give his exact statistics. He asserted that the reason why the Angora goat degenerated, whenever the attempt was made to naturalise it elsewhere, was that the secret of breeding was unknown, and the goats were kept studiously pure in breed, instead of being strengthened by regular recurrence to the fundamental stock.

I believe, therefore, that the breeding of the Angora goat, the Laodicean sheep, and the Colossian sheep, are secrets inherited by the Turks from the old people of Asia Minor. I have found two inscriptions of Pessinus, mentioning gifts of tunics, socks, etc., sent to the Emperor Trajan by a Galatian lady :[1] the socks which she thought worth sending to the Roman Emperor were probably similar to those glossy beautiful socks of Angora wool, which are still sold at Sivri-Hissar,[2] for she would not send such articles, unless there were something remarkable and unique about them.

One curious illustration of the continuity of customs and ways from pre-Turkish time down to the present day is furnished by St. Jerome. He draws a contrast between the Arabs, who eat locusts, and the natives of Phrygia or Pontus, who would regard it as an unnatural thing if they were forced to eat a locust.[3] The same contrast impresses the traveller at the present day : the people of Anatolia regard the locust, or the idea of eating it, with horror, but the Arabs feed with relish on locusts. Sir Charles Wilson pointed out this contrast to me many years ago. Now this aversion to a food, which is declared to be perfectly wholesome, is not likely to have been originally shared in by the Turks, a barbarous people coming from a country where food was scarce. This little trait

---

[1] Still unpublished.   [2] See p. 201.

[3] "Compelle Phrygem et Ponticum ut locustam comedat, nefas putabit," *Adv. Jovin.*, ii., 7.

is typical of many, which force all the travellers known to me, who have been most familiar with Asia Minor, to the conclusion that the so-called Turkish people of that country is fundamentally the ancient Anatolian population, into which the Turkish conquerors have melted, affecting it doubtless to some extent in the process, but disappearing in it, while they affected it.

As I have begun to speak of locusts, this chapter may be concluded by a few words about the periodical appearance of that scourge of the country, which devastated Asia Minor for several years previous to 1882, and caused great suffering, and which came much before our eyes in 1880 and 1881. The belief throughout the country is that the locusts die out after the seventh year from natural causes; and, certainly, they were seen no more after 1882. The time when they do most harm is when they are young, before they develop wings. In the earlier stage they march over the country in armies of incalculable numbers, and leave behind them nothing green. " The locusts have no king, yet they go forth all of them by bands." In the years of the plague, you might often ride across an army on the march. They seemed, as a rule, to go in a column about seventy to eighty yards broad or less; but of the length from van to rear I can give no estimate. The sides of the column are as clearly defined as

the flanks of a column of soldiers. Near Smyrna
I saw an army whose line of march happened for a
short distance to touch and coincide in direction
with a road : at that part the left half of the road
and the fields beside it were black with locusts,
while the right half had not a single locust on it.
No locust stops or swerves either to right or left,
but each marches by a series of jumps straight on,
till he finds something green to eat, which millions
devour in a few seconds ; while the rest pour on
over them, and the onward march is thus never
interrupted for a moment. If a wall or a house or
a city comes in their way, they go right over it, up
the one side and down the other.

When we were at Angora in 1881, the country
round, especially to the west and south, was
ravaged by them, and we rode across many armies
of them. In the city they swarmed in streets and
houses alike; when you poured some water into
a tumbler to drink, out tumbled several locusts
from the porous terra-cotta jug in which for the
sake of coolness the water is kept; when you
turned down the bed-clothes you disclosed a lot
of locusts ; when you felt something moving in your
sleeve or your trouser-leg, it was a locust. They
choked up the fountains and impeded the streams.
The British consul was active in promoting measures
against the scourge. The population of the country

was ordered out *en masse* against them. Every village was required to give proof of having buried a weight of locusts proportionate to the population. When I mention, on the authority of the consul, what the total result was, most people, I find, consider that either the consul or I was competing with Baron Munchausen: he declared that official statistics showed a total weight of 1620 tons buried in the province. All that I can say is that it would be difficult to imagine that things could have been worse, if the 1620 tons had been left alive.

Armies of locusts are always followed by the locust-bird, a beautiful bird with bright and varied plumage, which feeds upon them. It is never seen in Asia Minor, except when the locusts are there.

When the locusts get wings they fly away, alighting to feed in an erratic way at long intervals. Thus the country is not devastated in such a complete and continuous style. They fly, as I have been assured by good observers, always against the wind. I have only once seen an army flying, and on that occasion the light of day was darkened for a long time. It is said that near the sea coast, if the wind sets in towards the land, the locusts fly against it out to sea, drop in, and are drowned in whole armies. In the summer of 1880, I saw on the Ionian coast, near Erythrae, a continuous pile of dead locusts, near two feet high, along the edge of the sea for more than a mile, as they had been washed up by the waves and driven in by the steady sea-breeze that blows every afternoon for hours. How far the pile extended I know not, as we turned away. The stench was exceedingly disagreeable.

The belief throughout the country is that the plague of locusts lasts only seven years, and then stops. The year 1882 was, I think, only the fifth year of the plague ; but it proved the last. In Smyrna, in the middle of May, people were already congratulating themselves on their deliverance ; the locusts, after being born and beginning their march in spring, in the usual way, seemed to be affected by some kind of disease, and died in myriads. It was said that their bodies were discoloured ; but I cannot speak as an eye-witness of this. I have never seen a locust again in any part of the country. The question is worth consideration, whether the disease is developed by over-population : when the locusts are too crowded, insanitary conditions are perhaps responsible for the disease. If that be so, the active policy which wars against the locusts and thins them out, would really be a means of perpetuating the scourge ; and the wise policy would be to let them increase as rapidly as they tend to—a triumph for the Turkish system. It is certain that the locusts maintained

themselves in Cyprus for many years against all
the efforts of the British administration to exter-
minate them, whereas they soon died out in Asia
Minor. Those who are better informed on the
subject will probably be able to answer the question that I have put.

CHAPTER XII.

TIPS TO ARCHÆOLOGICAL TRAVELLERS.

MANY hints to travellers are contained in the earlier chapters ; and the following notes, while dealing specially with the method of travelling usefully and easily, may be found also to throw some light on the people and the state of the country.

It is possible to travel with very various degrees of equipment and following. In what is here said on the subject, regard is had solely to the traveller who aims at archæological and topographical study, and desires to do as much as possible in a short time. I have experimented in various styles, and the result is the two rules—(1) take of luggage as little as possible ; your happiness is inversely proportionate to the amount that you have to pack (unless you have a useful valet, an experiment which I did not make) ; (2) any baggage should be sent under charge of a servant, while the archæologist rides with one or more servants in quest of discoveries.

As to baggage, it is worth while travelling in a barbarous country to learn how unnecessary many of the supposed " necessities " of life are.   One or more servants are an absolute necessity.   It is best to take at least one Mohammedan with you everywhere ; my experiments occasionally with a Christian servant only showed that the method has some disadvantages.   Especially in a city like Afiom-Kara-Hissar, it is not advisable to go about antiquity-hunting alone.   In June, 1881, I spent a few days there when travelling with Sir Charles Wilson.   On the day after our arrival I went out alone to seek for inscriptions.   A knot of people soon began to follow.   When I stopped to copy an inscription in the doorway of a mosque, the knot grew into a large crowd, which pushed and struggled and blocked the light, and began after a time to look so threatening, that I felt it prudent to get away.   One of Sir C. Wilson's men was told off to look after me in future, and I was not again troubled, even when looking through the vast cemeteries, which surround this and every other Turkish town.

It is not easy to get a really good and useful servant.   The only thoroughly useful servant whom I ever had is described on p. 47 f. ; and I believe him to have had Kurd blood in him.   Turks are as a rule so stupid, handless, and incapable, as to be of little or no use in the most important parts of the work.   The best of them whom I have known has his portrait drawn on p. 45. Albanians are far more intelligent and useful than Turks; and, as a rule, the traveller has most chance of doing well with an Albanian (*Arnaout*). They have some faults of flightiness, and they are prone to take a lofty view of their own importance; but, so long as you keep a tight hand on them, this latter quality may be turned very much to your own advantage. In exaggerating his own importance, the Albanian necessarily gives a correspondingly exaggerated picture of his master's consequence. When you have an Albanian with you, the respect paid to you by the Turks during your earlier journeys will always be greater than when you have only Turks, or Turks and Greeks, as servants; and, if you know enough of the native languages to be able to elicit the reason (which most archæologists cannot do), you will find that a very interesting picture and history of yourself has been disseminated.

In October, 1881, we were received in Sandykli with extraordinary civility and respect. The *kaimmakam* himself came to pay us a visit, before we had sent to report ourselves to him—an unexampled honour to an ordinary traveller, and strictly contrary to etiquette and rule, of which the officials usually are very tenacious. He found us established in a khan; and at once insisted that such a place was entirely unsuitable for us to live in. He placed at our disposal a good house, which was temporarily vacant in the absence of the owner and his family, persons evidently of means and standing in the city; and he conducted us personally to the house, and showed the most obsequious and respectful attention. I could not understand the situation, until I found that our Albanian Akhmet had published through the whole bazaar, before we had been half an hour in Sandy-kli, that the son of the Valide Sultana of Inghil-terra had arrived with his harem and an English aide-de-camp. It was too late to do anything to correct the error; but I warned Akhmet that he must in future draw it milder.

For a long journey, lasting several months during the summer, it is advantageous to have a tent, especially for beginners. In the first place, it is more imposing: a traveller with tent and horses and servants is obviously a person of consequence. Now it is extremely important for your purpose that this impression should be spread around; and a servant who can trumpet abroad your importance is always more useful. It is also more cleanly and enjoyable, though when a sudden thunderstorm comes on it is unpleasant to sit up in bed under an umbrella, and try to keep a waterproof sheet over the bedding; and if a violent wind rises, it is almost as bad to rush out and pile large stones on the ends of the canvas lest the tent be blown away.

Further, unless all the archæologists be exceedingly affable, you don't see much of the natives, if you live in a tent.

Most of my journeys were done in this way; but other methods of travel more simple and economical may be practised. In September and October, 1881, when my friend, Professor Sterrett, had to leave for Smyrna, I tried an experiment in economy, travelling with a single servant and one baggage horse. The following twenty-four days were a miserable time. The baggage horse, a fine animal with a light load, was frisky and constantly straying. We were not skilled in balancing his load, and it kept shifting. Our time was spent, not in seeking monuments, but in minding that horse and rebalancing his load. If we heard of inscriptions an hour away to the right or left, we could not go to them, being bound to our pack-horse. On the second day he ran off, and we pursued; it was a comic spectacle to see his load dance uneasily over his back for some time, and at last slide round and settle in a tangled mass between his legs. We nearly fell off our own steeds laughing as that horse stopped, embarrassed by the unusual position of his load, and looked helplessly around; but our laugh was changed to wailing when we had to spend half an hour re-packing and reloading. We should have been better off, and done far more work, if we had had no baggage except saddle-bags on our own horses. You can turn on the natives to cook for you in an evening, and they will do so with the greatest pleasure as soon as they realise that you provide the meat and they the cooking, for a meal all round.

You must have your whole day, and one or more servants, free for archæologising ; and you cannot combine that with minding baggage. With two mounted servants you can do many things that are not possible with one. For example, you see two villages two or three miles from each other : you go to one, and send a man to the other. The latter has been trained to recognise what you want ; and is able to report whether the village deserves a visit. With three servants, as my wife and I had in 1884 after Mr. A. H. Smith was invalided, one can sweep a great valley from end to end in marvellously short time.

A few words about the humble but absolutely necessary department of the commissariat will not be beneath the dignity of future archæologists. You can't work without food ; and food is perfectly easy to procure, if you know how to arrange ; but, if you do not go about it in the proper way and are unable to speak to the natives, you may come near starving, as was the case in that brief and unfortunate journey, which the "Wandering Scholar" describes in amusing and pathetic terms in the second chapter of his entertaining book.

It is a wise rule always to have with you, attached to your own saddle (either in saddle-bags, or a pocket connected with the saddle) a small supply of preserved food : I have found a tin of sardines handy to carry, and a useful change from the ordinary inland food. If you are benighted, or fail to reach camp, you have then always a stand-by, which relieves you of a pressing anxiety. This rule should never be neglected : you may carry the same tin for a month without using it, but never omit it. When one is working long hours, and trying to traverse as much ground as possible, sunset has a habit of coming down in a most awkward manner.

Scores of times I have had a long ride of one or two hours in black darkness on a strange road, in complete uncertainty as to the way. Sometimes we came out at the wrong village, generally at the right one; occasionally we had to lie out on the open ground and wait till morning. Until I made the sardine rule absolute, such rides in the dark were a time of anxiety : with a tin of sardines you are master of your fate. In November, 1881, among the Phrygian mountains, my wife and I found ourselves alone in a pitch-dark night, two hours from our village, probably on the wrong road. It was hard frost, the altitude was 3900 feet above sea, the prospect was discouraging, but it seemed best to go on, as behind lay forest and steep ground down which we had with some difficulty made our way in the gloaming. After a time we saw a distant light away to the left. We made a bee-line for that light ; it shone from a house in our village that stood high on a hill with a door facing in our direction and standing open ; and near the village we met our men, who had missed us in the forest owing to their dilatoriness, and, after returning home alone, came out in alarm to search for us. When I came to know the valley better, I found we had ridden across a great marsh, which was impassable through most of the year, but was frozen hard in November ; and the road, on which we had been, led to no village. That was the worst of many narrow escapes from a night in the open country : in summer this is no great hardship, and with sardines, servants, and a fire is a mere picnic.

Apart from accidents, you sometimes find near sunset that the camp is in one direction and a tempting inscription is reported in the other. Armed with your tin of sardines you prefer the latter : without it you must return to camp.

An excellent rule is to have your dinner for the

evening purchased in the morning before camp is moved, and transported in the baggage. The natives are very loath to do this, partly from the unvarying law in Turkey never to do what can be postponed for a little, partly from the fixed belief that meat must be cooked within an hour or two after being killed. But this is a popular fallacy: in the fine clear air of the upper plateau, a lamb used to last four days' dinner for a small camp, and was eatable on the fourth occasion (at least to hungry men). Always, therefore, compel your men to buy a fowl, or something else, in the morning: in a town get lamb or kid. Sheep or goat of the second year is uneatable to an archæologist, though Turks or Turkmens prefer the larger animal to the smaller. Lamb of six weeks old tastes, not like our lamb, but like delicate mutton.

Fish are rarely found, and when found are usually bad: the natives usually have a prejudice against fish, and my own experience has been unfavourable. Fish of considerable size swarm in the Porsuk-Su (Tembris), a tributary of the Sangarios, but are flabby and taste like mud; two hungry archæologists, after a mouthful or two of such a fish, could eat no more. In the clear, sparkling, mountain stream that flows through the Taurus by Bozanti Khan (on the pass leading south to the Cilician Gates), a small kind of fish is caught; I had a most violent attack of sickness in 1891 after eating some of them, and so had all who partook. These are perhaps the same fish of which the Arab historian Maçoudi tells a strange story (*Les Prairies d'Or*, vii., p. 97).

Returning from an expedition into the Byzantine territory, the Khalif Mamoun encamped by the side of the beautiful stream, whose waters were so clear that the legend on a silver coin, which was thrown in, could be read as it lay at the bottom, and so cold that it was impossible to bathe in them.   Mamoun saw a fine fish in the water, and promised a reward to the man who should bring it to him.   A servant caught it ; but, as he was handing it to the Khalif, the fish slipped out of his hand back into the stream, and splashed the ice-cold water over the royal robes. The fish was again caught ; but hardly had the order been given that it should be fried, when the Khalif was seized with a chill, and began to tremble like a leaf.   His attendants covered him with garments and lit a fire ; but he continued to complain of the cold, and when the fish was brought cooked to him, he could not eat it.   He asked the name of the stream : it was called Koshaira, " stretch out thy feet ".   He asked the name of the district : it was called Rakha.   Then he remembered the prophecy that he was to die at a place called

Rakha, on which account he had always avoided the city of that name. That night he died; and Moutassem, his brother, reigned in his stead, and carried his body to Tarsus, and buried it there.

In the upper waters of the Hermus alone, where it is a clear mountain stream, have fish been caught which have produced no ill consequences in my experience; but even they are not specially good eating.

A camp-bed is a comfort, and conducive to health; but it adds considerably to the baggage. Some years I carried one with me; in other years I have left it in Smyrna. By doing without it, and sleeping on the ground for months, I learned to understand a passage in Catullus's famous Ode 31. Some of the commentators have vexed themselves to explain by bad illustrative passages why, as soon as he caught sight of his home, Catullus thought of "the bed desired so long". Let them make a coasting voyage in a tiny yacht like Catullus's through the Ægean sea, and lie as hard as he must have lain on the planks, and they will appreciate his point of view. Further, they will cease to have the doubts which some of them feel, whether the voyage described in 4, and looked back upon in 31, was real or imaginary. You have all the stages of the true traveller's experience: in 46 the itch to wander (as Sir Th. Martin renders it):—

> Already through each nerve a flutter runs
>   Of eager hope, that longs to be away;
> Already 'neath the light of other suns
>   My feet, new-wing'd for travel, yearn to stray;

in 31 the longing that has grown as time passes for a comfortable bed; in 4 the pleasure in recalling past adventures and in associating them with the inanimate friend that bore him through them.

After sleeping for months on the ground, I came once to the city of Ushak, where I had an introduction to a wealthy Turkish family of five brothers, carpet manufacturers. After supper, when I expressed a wish to sleep, the youngest of the brothers brought in two large mattresses, soft and springy, each a foot thick, laid one above the other, spread silk sheets over them and a coverlet on top: then all bade good-night. I took off my thick jacket and sat down on the side of the mattresses to enjoy for a moment the pleasure of sitting soft and warm (the season was late, chill October); but my head sank on the bed, and I knew nothing till the morning sun wakened me. To my extreme disgust I had missed the comfort provided for me, falling asleep in my clothes with my feet in heavy wet boots resting on the floor. But I shall never forget the exquisite sensation of sinking on that soft couch; and yet, in ordinary circumstances, a soft mattress, or the old-fashioned feather-bed, is an abomination to me and the sure cause of a sleepless night.

It is absolutely necessary to carry warm clothing with one at all periods of the year. In June there is often a cold and rainy week or two, especially in the mountains: in the end of July I have experienced two days of rain, wind and cold in the Anti-Taurus region, which is very high ; in the first half of July, even among the lower Phrygian mountains, I have once known a similar storm (chapter iii.). Moreover, the evenings are almost always chilly, when you are above 3000 feet ; and, if you sit in the open air, as we usually did, you must have a warm greatcoat to put on. In the cities, where the mud houses get saturated with heat during the day, and radiate it during the evening, the interiors are most stuffy and oppressive after sunset. On the open plains, the soil, having been baked by the sun for fifteen hours, is near red-hot in the late afternoon ; and, if you put up a tent then, it keeps in the heat and retains it for many hours ; but I preferred to open the tent all round in the early evening, so as to let the ground and the air inside grow cool. After some years' experience, I began the habit of carrying on my saddle, not merely a waterproof cloak (which is quite indispensable at all times on the plateau, owing to the sudden, heavy thunderstorms), but also a thick greatcoat ;

and I have often had to put on both to keep myself from starving of cold, though my travelling on the plateau only once lasted later than 20th October, and usually began not much before the last week of May.

Most of the inscribed stones that have as yet been discovered in the Turkish country are found either in cemeteries, or in the walls of mosques, or in the masonry of the fountains which are often the least squalid erections in a Turkish village. The travelling archæologist can, and ought to, make sure of omitting none of the inscribed stones in these three classes; and yet it is marvellous how difficult it is to induce most travellers to examine patiently every one of these places in every village. I could tell many stories on this subject, some of them heart-rending tales of lost opportunities, some of them hair-breadth escapes from such losses; but the most striking incidents of this kind might cause some regret, and I do not wish to recall them.

In the houses or huts of the Turks, there is less need for good stones than in the more elaborate structure of mosques and fountains; but even in the poorest hut a fine old inscription may be concealed,[1] and in the best houses inscribed

---

[1] An example, p. 120.

marbles are often found. For stones in private houses or in barns, on *tchiftliks*, the archæologist must trust to chance, or the favour of heaven, or his own wit and power of ingratiating himself with the natives (as described in the first two chapters), or a smart servant (if he is lucky enough to find one). Time is needed to make discoveries in this direction, and it is quite certain that in the greater cities, like Kara-Hissar, Konia, Kutaya, and many others, there remains a great deal to reward the archæologists of the future. But they must be prepared to spend time; and with the railways that now spread so far over Asia Minor, they can travel in a day into the heart of the country, and settle there at a city in comparative ease of a rough and ready kind. The explorer must not, however, expect a European hotel. He must be prepared to use his own wit to fill his own stomach; or he will often fare very badly. I have known of a large party of archæologists starving in a village by the sea-coast, where they were stationed for some time, barely keeping themselves alive on bread and boiled weeds, with an occasional egg on lucky days, until one after another they were all struck down by fever resulting from lowness of the system; and yet there were numberless flocks of sheep not far away, as well as fowls in the village. But none of the party could talk Greek, or put their needs and resolves before the people ; and so they contented themselves with sending to Smyrna for tins of beef from Paraguay, or salmon from Canada, which always went astray in transit. If you prefer to be idle, you can starve anywhere in Asia Minor outside of Smyrna.

Inscribed stones are commonly turned upside down. The reason probably is that the letters frequently cover only half or less of the stone ; and it seems more suitable to the illiterate eye to put these irregular markings close to the ground, and to have the smooth part in the more conspicuous place. This is a fruitful cause of trouble, and error, to the archæologist. It is far harder to read correctly, when you have to put your head where your feet should be.

In the first years of my work in Asia Minor, I always tried to make the best of the stone as it was ; but in 1883 my companion, Professor Sterrett, showed me the error of my ways. With true American power of subduing nature, he pointed out that the wise man instead of adapting his position to the stone, would adapt the stone to himself. Some stones are fixed immovably; others seem to be fixed ; but it is marvellous how many can be turned straight at the mention of the potent word *bakshish.*

One word more of advice. Never pay a man

until the end of his service; dangle always before his eyes the prospect of pay and extra reward (*bakshish*) at the end of his time, but give him nothing beforehand.   It may ruin the best Oriental to get any reward during his term of work.